"I have just lost my girl. I still need a wife."

Her heart banged against her ribs, and her breath came in shallow gasps. If he mentioned a marriage of convenience, she would hit him.

"I have been out of the country for five years. I am not familiar with the new crop of debs. Which of them would suit my purpose? Mama mentioned Lady Sara Winsley."

"Oh," she said. It was a sigh of regret.

"My mind is not quite made up."

"Then allow me to mention my own special friend, Miss Sutton."

"Let us include a third. We require a Venus, as well as a Hera and Athena. God, what a conceited ass I am."

"Yes, aren't you?" she replied tartly.

"Thus far, we have only selected two." His lips quirked in a pensive smile. "But our wits have gone begging. You must be the third."

"You won't have any trouble finding a third lady willing to make a fool of herself over you. I am not interested."

Also by Joan Smith
Published by Fawcett Books:

THE NOTORIOUS LORD HAVERGAL
BATH SCANDAL
JENNIE KISSED ME
THE BAREFOOT BARONESS
DANGEROUS DALLIANCE
FRANCESCA
WIFE ERRANT
THE SPANISH LADY
GATHER YE ROSEBUDS

THE SAVAGE
LORD GRIFFIN

Joan Smith

FAWCETT CREST • NEW YORK

Sale of this book without a front cover may be unauthorized. If this book is coverless, it may have been reported to the publisher as "unsold or destroyed" and neither the author nor the publisher may have received payment for it.

A Fawcett Crest Book
Published by Ballantine Books
Copyright © 1993 by Joan Smith

All rights reserved under International and Pan-American Copyright Conventions. Published in the United States of America by Ballantine Books, a division of Random House, Inc., New York, and simultaneously in Canada by Random House of Canada Limited, Toronto.

Library of Congress Catalog Card Number: 93-90195

ISBN 0-449-22016-8

Manufactured in the United States of America

First Edition: September 1993

Chapter One

The Duke of Dunsmore charged into his fiancée's saloon on Berkeley Square, his eyes starting from their sockets, to make him appear even more witless than usual.

"Myra, I have just heard the most awful thing!" he exclaimed, in an epicene bleat. The duke stood near the summit of society, but he stood on the shoulders of giants. It was his influential family and his vast fortune that accounted for his preeminent position. Neither his talents, his looks, nor his industry were sufficient to raise him above the rank of valet.

The three Newbold ladies stared at him in alarm. His fiancée's mama, Mrs. Newbold, was the first to recover and demand to know what he was talking about. "The duchess has come to town!" she said, and fell back against the sofa cushions in dismay. This was a polite way of saying that the duke's wedding to her elder daughter was off. The duchess had been safely tucked away at her castle in Scotland during Myra's courting of the duke. It was assumed the mama had some more eligible lady in her eye for her eldest son.

"Eh?" Dunsmore said in confusion. "No such a thing."

The color seeped back into Mrs. Newbold's blanched cheeks. "You frightened the life out of me, Duke," she said, attempting a smile. "Whatever has you in such a pelter?" Her next thought was that Bonaparte had escaped again. She could accept this minor disaster without flinching.

"Griffin is back!" the duke gasped, and stumbled to the sofa, where he sat, panting, and clinging to Myra's fingers.

"Oh no!" Myra said in a strangled whisper.

"Impossible!" Mrs. Newbold exclaimed.

"Is he *really*?" Miss Alice said, with a trembling smile of joy.

"I heard it on Bond Street just now," the duke assured them. "They say he looked like a wild beast when he lunged down the gangplank of the ship that brought him home. It was a Royal Navy vessel. His skin had turned black, his hair was down to his shoulders, he was carrying a spear and leading an orangutan on a chain. What are we to do?"

His Grace looked helplessly from his fiancée to her mama. He was not one to court excitement, and took no pleasure from the sensation his announcement caused. Questions were fired at the poor man's head until he hardly knew whether he was coming or going. He could not tell them where Lord Griffin had been, or how he had revived from the dead and reached England, but on one dismal point he was certain. Griffin was back.

"Just like Robinson Crusoe!" Alice said, and received three rebukeful glares.

"Griffin was not shipwrecked on a desert island, Alice," her mama informed her, "though it would have been just like him. We knew he reached Brazil. I felt at the time he went that he had no business sheering off when he had just offered for Myra."

"And she accepted him," Alice pointed out, with a mischievous glance at Dunsmore.

"But that was five years ago!" Myra wailed. "He is supposed to be dead. No word for over four years. He never wrote a single line after the first few months. I was sure cannibals had eaten him, or some such thing," she said with an air of injury.

"It is pretty clear to me he hasn't a case to stand on," the duke said. "What did he say in his last letter?"

"He said he was trying to get someone to take him to the Amazon jungle."

"They don't grow coffee in the Amazon jungle, do they?" the duke asked. "Was that not why he went to Brazil, to set up a coffee plantation?"

"No, no," Alice said. "He was going to collect specimens for his botanical garden. You know how the Griffins have always loved horticulture. He only told the government people he was interested in coffee to facilitate getting his passport validated. Dom John was encouraging that sort of settlement, you must know."

Her listeners' blinks of confusion told her they knew nothing of the sort.

"Who the deuce is Dom John?" the duke asked.

"He is the Prince Regent," Alice told him.

"Eh? No such a thing. Prinny's name is George, not Dom John."

"The Prince Regent of Portugal. He sought refuge in Brazil when Bonaparte invaded Portugal. He is eager to get industry going in Brazil. Do you not read the journals, Duke?"

"I read something about it," Dunsmore said

3

vaguely. "Of more importance, what are we to do about Griffin?"

"You won't have to do anything, Duke," Alice said. "Griffin will marry Myra."

Mrs. Newbold gave her younger daughter a murderous glare and said, "Hush up, you foolish child."

Myra squeezed her fiancé's ineffectual fingers and said, "You will have to tell him that I am marrying you, dear."

The duke, no model of manliness at the best of times, looked like a frightened rooster. His hair was a lank, lackluster blond, his skin pale, and his eyes a watery blue. He was a tall, ungainly concern. Neither Weston's tailoring nor his valet's grooming could make his six feet of skin and bones look better than merely passable.

Alice would have felt sorry for him, if her attention had not been directed at her sister. How could Myra prefer this man milliner to Griffin? It was incomprehensible how her sister could have agreed to marry two such different gentlemen.

Griffin was a regular corsair—tall, dark, outrageously handsome, dashing, and daring. Dunsmore, on the other hand, was a fool. But an extremely wealthy fool, of course, and a duke to boot. Competition had been fierce to become the next Duchess of Dunsmore. Five years was a long time to wait for a fiancé, and Myra had been peeved with Griffin for going to Brazil in the first place. If it had been *her*, Alice thought to herself, she would have rushed the wedding forward and gone to Brazil with him, as he wanted.

Myra had been only seventeen at the time; Mama thought seventeen too young to marry. She also thought it just as well that Griffin leave the country until it was time for the wedding. She trusted her daugher implicitly, but she did not trust the dashing

4

Griffin an inch where ladies were concerned. Mersham Abbey, Griffin's country seat, was adjacent to Newbold Hall in Kent.

Myra had been faithful to her memories for five years. The mischief only occurred during the last month, when Alice was taken to London to make her debut. Myra had come along, of course, and was the acknowledged belle of the Season. Her romantic history and her beauty had caught society's imagination, and before she knew it, she had caught the duke. All the attention had gone to her head. There was no point denying Myra had changed. She gloried in her newfound attention, and seemed determined to make up for those five wasted years.

Mrs. Newbold's mind was running in other channels. She had just thought of another tremendous problem. Griffin's cousin and heir, Lloyd Montgomery, had already taken over Mersham Abbey. "I wonder if Monty knows," she said.

"Oh, it is too horrid!" Myra exclaimed, stamping her dainty foot. "Griffin is spoiling everything. My wedding is only a month away. You must speak to him, Duke, and tell him I am marrying you. I don't want him coming here, pestering me."

"Surely he would not expect you to have waited five years," Mrs. Newbold said, but she said it doubtfully.

"He will certainly call on his fiancée at least," Alice assured them. "Unless he has married someone else himself in the meanwhile," she added uncertainly.

"Who would there be to marry in Brazil?" her mama asked. "Nothing but pickaninnies."

"Oh, Mama! Don't be a peagoose," Alice said. "All the Portuguese nobles are there. Their court has moved to Rio de Janeiro."

"Where do you hear such things?" her mama asked, with a frown of disapproval.

"I read the journals, Mama." She had read any article on Brazil with particular interest since Griffin's departure. Although she had barely reached her teens when he left, she had not been too young to succumb to his charms. Many a night she lay awake, imagining Griffin had chosen her, instead of Myra. And now he was back! Myra was engaged to the duke—any wonderful thing seemed possible.

"Perhaps he hasn't written to me because he is married, and is ashamed of himself," Myra said hopefully. "Did you hear Griffin was alone when he jumped down the gangplank, Duke?"

"No, he was with a 'rangutan. I did not hear he had a lady with him. It would have been mentioned."

"You had best go to him right away, Duke," Myra said, rising to hasten him off before Griffin should come, with his spear and long hair and ape, to terrorize her. She shivered to think of having to deal with such a ghastly apparition.

She had been flattered at his offer when she was young and foolish, but since meeting Dunsmore, she had come to realize what sort of gentleman just suited her. With Griffin, it had been the attraction of opposites; with the duke, it was like drawn to like. Dunsmore was quiet and easy to get along with. He never wanted her to go hunting, or urged her to take the reins of his curricle. Indeed, he did not like the open carriage at all. He did not pester her with talk of philosophy or politics, except for the Corn Laws. He was on a government committee studying the Corn Laws. Certainly he would never ask her to go sailing off to Brazil. He was a real gentleman.

The duke rose and stood, wiping his chin with his

long fingers. "Yes, quite. Er—what should I say, Myra?"

"Tell him we are being married next month."

"That is inviting slaughter. I mean if he insists he still wants to marry you . . . I mean to say—you were engaged to him first."

Myra's pretty face screwed up. She threw herself on Dunsmore's chest as the tears gathered in her eyes. "Oh, Dunny, you must not let him come here! I could not bear it!"

Alice crossed her arms and watched the performance, then said impatiently, "For goodness' sake, Myra! He cannot *make* you marry him. Tell him you have changed your mind, if you have." Her scathing glance at the duke spoke of her own feelings in the matter. "I daresay someone has told him by now that you are marrying Dunsmore. It has been announced in all the journals."

"That is true!" Myra said, blinking through a mist of tears at her duke. "It is the talk of the town."

"The thing to do," the duke said, adopting a firm stance, "just sit tight and do nothing. Wait and see what Griffin does. Mean to say—he will have read the papers. Next move is up to him."

Myra nodded, happy to spare the duke such misery as a confrontation with the awful Griffin. "But if he tries to see me, Dunny, you must be here to stand by me, or there is no saying what will happen." She had indeed no clear picture of what Griffin might do, but that spear featured in it somewhere.

"We could make a dart to Dunsmore Castle," he suggested shamelessly.

Myra considered this a moment. "Scotland is so far away, and we are to be married at St. George's on Hanover Square next month. I have my wedding clothes being fitted . . . No, we shall stay and confront him, Dunny." She squared her shoulders and smiled bravely at the duke. "After all, Griffin is a gentleman."

"Or was," the duke said less bravely, thinking of that spear. He envisaged it as being six feet long at least, one end festooned with feathers, the other dripping with blood.

He took his leave, promising to return for dinner. He spent the remainder of the afternoon at Manton's shooting gallery in Davies Street, purchasing a gun and trying his hand at a wafer. His ears rang from the explosions, and his lungs burned from the smoke. He did not hit a single wafer, but he shot out a window and narrowly missed shooting Joe Manton. Manton said, when the duke left, that he had seen many poor shots in his life, but he had never before seen a man who did not know which end of the pistol the bullet came out of.

Myra and her mama drove by the back streets to the modiste who was doing Myra's wedding clothes. They took three armed footmen with them, and drew the curtains of their carriage, congratulating themselves that it was not the same carriage they had when Griffin left, and he would never know to see it that it was theirs. They made it safely to the modiste and back without attack. Upon their return, Alice informed them that Griffin had not called.

She had spent a weary afternoon looking out the front window, waiting. She hoped Griffin would come when she was alone, so that she might give him a picture of how things now stood, to save him the pain of Myra's defection. In her romantic young mind, she envisaged his eyes steaming into hers, as he realized that it was her he had loved all the time. Indeed, he had only stayed in Brazil because he could not jilt Myra. As soon as the jungle drums had brought word of her betrothal, he hopped the first frigate home to claim his true love.

Lord Griffin spent the day incommunicado at his London residence, being shaved and shorn and fitted for a new jacket. He wanted to look his best to reclaim his fiancée. He did not read any journals, or entertain any callers who enlightened him as to her recent doings. He spoke to a few specialists in botany, but they were not members of the *ton*. Their conversation had to do solely with horticulture. It was not until that evening that he called at Berkeley Square and turned the Newbolds' life all topsy-turvy.

Chapter Two

The Newbolds' evening had been arranged a week in advance. They were hosting a small dinner party, after which they would make early stops at two routs, before proceeding to Lady Calmet's grand ball, where they would dance till dawn. The Season was ending on a high note as proud mamas flaunted their daughters' catch, or in Lady Calmet's case, as a frustrated mama made one last desperate push to nab a son-in-law.

As the girls had the finishing touches put on their toilettes, Alice studied her sister for signs of dangerous beauty. Myra was a spineless creature, but she was undeniably pretty. Her golden hair was stylishly arranged in a bundle of curls high on her head, to show off her swan-like neck. Her blue eyes sparkled, and her pale coloring was heightened by the excitement of Griffin's return. No one ever bothered to look for a flaw in her gowns. She was quite an acknowledged pattern-card of fashion. On this evening she wore an ice-blue gown with small spangles arranged in a wave design, rising and falling at intervals, around the bottom of her skirt. The wave shape was her own invention, and would undoubtedly have started a new fashion, were the Season not so close to being over.

Alice turned to the mirror and was unhappy with the image staring back at her. She looked like a wildflower set against that rare, cultivated rose, Myra. Her thick chestnut hair had no notion of staying where her dresser put it. They had long since given up on trying to introduce a ribbon or a bow into it. It jettisoned such alien matter in minutes. The only thing in its favor was that it had a natural curl, but an active curl that bounced and hopped about in a most unladylike manner. Her face was a perfect heart in shape, diminishing to a chin that Alice felt was too small. Her wide mouth required a generous jaw and chin. Alice stoutly maintained that she did not possess a single good feature, but if pressed, she would say with no enthusiasm that she supposed her eyes were all right. They were brown, and had generous enough lashes.

Her boyish figure showed to best advantage in the saddle. The white ball gowns she was obliged to wear in her first Season did nothing for her, and vice versa. The pink bows had a way of sagging even before her busy fingers pulled them to pieces, and it was taken for granted that the gown would come home with a dusty bottom and wine spilled down the front of it. With all these disadvantages, it surprised everyone that she had an ardent circle of admirers. Those young gentlemen on their first Season who were afraid of real ladies felt at home to a peg with Alice. It was not every girl who laughed good-naturedly when you trod on her toes, or who could handle the ribbons as well as a man.

All through dinner the Newbolds and the duke were on thorns, waiting for Griffin to pounce in and

11

challenge the duke to a duel. He was the sole subject of conversation over dinner. Mrs. Winters heard he had brought a snow-white monkey back with him, and had trained it to speak. Unfortunately, it spoke Portuguese, or some foreign gibberish. Her husband heard Griffin had been hunting for diamonds in the Amazon, and had brought home a trunkful. But it was Mr. Barnaby, a neighbor from Kent, who caused the greatest sensation. He had been at the docks that afternoon, and had actually seen Griffin. In fact, it was Barnaby who had spread the tale of his appearance.

"He looked like a wild man, by God. I would not have recognized him in a million years. In fact, I tried to get away when I saw him coming at me, but he recognized me on the spot, and collared me. That fellow could outrun a hare."

"Is he really black?" Mrs. Newbold asked.

"No, he is bronze as an Indian, with hair streaming down to his shoulders. And he was carrying a long spear. He was given it by a tribe of pygmies in the Amazon."

"Then it must have been a small spear," the duke said hopefully.

"No, by God, it was as long as a barge pole, with a sharp point. He tells me the jungle Indians put some poison on the end of it that kills a man on contact."

Many eyes turned to the duke and Myra in sympathy or ill-concealed glee, depending on the looker's feelings.

"What about his orangutan?" Mrs. Newbold asked.

"No such a thing. What he had was a white monkey. An albino, he called it. A clever little rascal. It lifted my hat right off my head and flung it into the ocean. Griffin speared it out."

12

"At least Griffin did not use his spear on you," Alice said.

"I feared he would when I told him Montgomery had taken up residence at Mersham Abbey. You should have seen the black look he gave me. It was Monty's rushing Lady Griffin out of the abbey that got his dander up. I would not want to be in Monty's boots when Griffin goes home. Daresay he pelted straight off to the abbey to turn the fellow off."

A concerted sigh of relief was audible at the table. Myra and the duke exchanged a tremulous smile. Feeling that the confrontation had been staved off, the duke said, "Pity. I was hoping for a word with him before he left. Mean to say . . ."

"I recommend you have your word via letter," Mr. Barnaby suggested. "That lad's tongue can raise welts. I would not like to feel his fists."

When dinner was over and Griffin had still not come, it was generally accepted that he had darted straight off to Mersham Abbey to murder his cousin Montgomery, and the party could proceed to the rout with an easy mind. The story of Griffin's return was on every lip. The ladies, in particular, were extremely eager to see this handsome savage with his spear and trunkful of diamonds, and were sorry he had not returned at the beginning of the Season. They were soon to have at least a part of their wish.

At the Griffin mansion on Grosvenor Square, the only lingering trace of the jungle adorning Lord Griffin was his bronze coloring and a small gold hoop earring in one ear, which was exposed to view with his short hairdo. He thought this lent a certain diablerie to his appearance, but if Myra disliked it, he would remove it.

Always up to the minute in his toilette, he had

worn pantaloons before leaving England. His valet, who had gone to Brazil with his master but preceded Griffin to London by a week, had spoken to his confreres that afternoon regarding the important matters of tonsure and the cravat. Both were exquisitely arranged. Before his lordship was allowed to leave the house, his valet had overseen the clipping of his master's hair à la Brutus, and arranged his cravat in the Oriental fashion. The large diamond tiepin Griffin wore had been fashioned in Rio de Janeiro from the small stock of diamonds he had purchased at a ridiculously low price, and brought back with him.

It was an hour after the Newbolds and their party left for the rout that Griffin felt he was fit to be seen by his beloved, and directed John Groom to deliver him thither. The butler, seeing that the stories of Griffin's return to nature had been grossly exaggerated, did not hesitate to give him the Newbolds' evening itinerary. Neither did he feel it his place to inform his lordship that Miss Newbold had taken a new fiancé. He did drop one hint, however.

"Er, the ladies are accompanied by the Duke of Dunsmore," he said discreetly.

"Dunny? They shan't come to any harm with him—so long as they are not attacked by a ravening mouse," Griffin said, and left, smiling.

Naturally he did not expect Myra to sit on her thumbs for five years. He expected her to go about society, and lauded her mama's good sense in arranging such a harmless escort as the duke. Perhaps young Alice had attached Dunsmore. She must be old enough to be making her bows now. He had a vague memory of a dark-eyed young hussy tumbling about the house when he had been courting Myra.

It seemed strange to be back in London after such a long absence. Gas lamps had been installed since his departure, and he marveled at how they turned night into day. Lampposts stood at every corner, casting a misty glow on the passing carriages and pedestrians. Through the shadows, the series of lamps were visible along the street, like a cordon of moons come to earth. Amazing! But surely dangerous?

It was not until his carriage approached Lady Calmet's door that it occurred to him he had no invitation. He knew the family well, however. His mama and Lady Calmet had made their curtsies together three decades before. In fact, his mama was godmother to the daughter of the house. Sara, was it? He certainly would have been invited, had Lady Calmet known he was back. His heart beat faster as he approached the door. The butler stared, not recognizing Griffin, but recognizing him for a gentleman.

"Good evening. I am Lord Griffin. I don't have an invitation. I have been out of the country, but I am sure if you speak to Lady Calmet . . ."

Despite the lack of long locks and spear, the butler had no intention of coming to cuffs with the savage Lord Griffin. He stood aside and allowed Griffin to enter. Lord Calmet was just escaping to his study, and spotted Griffin as he fled.

"Good God, you're back, Griffin. Welcome," Calmet said, and pelted his guest with questions as he led him to the ballroom. "You must come for dinner soon, and tell us all about your adventures. Sara will be in alt to see you. Announce Lord Griffin," he said to the servant when they reached the landing that overlooked the ballroom.

"Thank you, milord." Griffin bowed and turned to the servant. "Wait!" he said, touching the man's elbow. "Let me just watch a moment." He smiled softly at the fairy-tale scene below him. Plumed and painted ladies swirled around the floor to a strangely seductive melody. He could discern no pattern to the dance. The squares of the cotillion or minuet were missing, yet there were no rows of a country-dance. It seemed to be a random arrangement of couples, each swooping and circling to its own will, with gentlemen actually holding their partners in their arms in public! What delightful depravity had struck London?

And soon he would be holding his lovely Myra. England had changed! "What is this new dance?" he asked.

"It is the waltz, milord."

"Charming," Griffin said, searching the floor for Myra, and just as happy not to find her in another man's arms. "You may announce me now."

"Lord Griffin," the servant called in a loud voice.

A hush fell over the ballroom. The waltzers stopped in mid-swirl. As the dancers halted, the music slowed to a discordant wail, then stopped entirely. Griffin had expected some little commotion at his return, but he had not expected this. He hardly knew what he should do. He smiled and bowed two or three times in different directions. When still no one moved a muscle, he found himself performing a tentative royal wave, as if he were the king. No further salutations occurred to him, and with a great sense of uncertainty, he began to walk down the stairs to the ballroom, looking this way and that for Myra.

His descent seemed to give the waltzers permission to return to life. A great, excited buzz broke out as he strolled past them.

"Handsome! Who said he wore his hair long?"

"I do not see any spear!"

16

"He can spear me any time he likes."

"What is that in his ear? It looks like—but it cannot be!"

"By Jove, I am glad I ain't Dunny Dunsmore," a man's voice said.

Lady Calmet, catapulted into motion when she recognized him, came rushing forward and grasped Griffin by both hands. "Dear boy! Such a pleasure! I did not half believe you were dead."

"Dead?" he asked, staring. "So that is why everyone looked as if they had seen a ghost. I was beginning to fear I had forgotten to put on my trousers."

"Oh, Griffin! You have not changed a bit," his hostess laughed.

"Indeed, I have not."

"Sara will be so glad to see you."

Griffin was a little surprised that both parents had mentioned Sara, but took it for mere politeness. "And I look forward to seeing her again, Lady Calmet. I was told at Newbolds' that Myra is here. Do you think you could steer us to a quiet parlor?"

Lady Calmet cast a strangely uneasy glance at him. "That might be best, Griffin. I shall have some wine sent in," she said, and led him out the door, to the consternation of every lady in the room except Myra Newbold, who was extremely relieved to see the back of him.

"Oh, Dunny!" Myra gasped. "He is here. Whatever shall we do?"

"We could make a bolt for it," he suggested.

Before they bolted, Lady Calmet came hurrying forward. "Lord Griffin would like a word with you in private, Myra," she said. "I'll take you to him."

"Oh no! I could not! Truly, I do not feel . . ."

Dunsmore drew a deep sigh of relief and said bracingly, "Must be done sooner or later, m'dear. As well to have it over with, eh?"

17

"You go with her, Dunsmore," Lady Calmet suggested, as she did not wish to have that ninnyhammer of a Myra Newbold faint away in the middle of the floor.

Alice watched from across the room, wishing with all her heart that Myra would turn tail and run, so that she might have the privilege of consoling Griffin. With all eyes upon her, however, Myra had enough backbone to allow Dunsmore and Lady Calmet to drag her to the private parlor. Her insides were shaking like a blancmange, and so were Dunsmore's. Lady Calmet thought they both looked as if they were going to meet the firing squad.

She tapped on the door, and Griffin opened it immediately. "Thank you, Lady Calmet," he said, but his eyes were devouring Myra. She was even more beautiful than he remembered. Her pale charms wore the added attraction of novelty, after his stay among natives. He took her hand and drew her inside. The duke tagged along.

Griffin said to him, "Thank you, Dunsmore, but there is no need—"

"Don't go, Dunny!" Myra begged in a low tone, clutching his arm.

"Matter of fact, there is need," Dunsmore said, and closed the door in Lady Calmet's face.

"What is it?" Griffin said impatiently.

The duke cleared his throat two or three times. "Thing is, Griffin, Myra and I—I mean to say, we thought you was dead."

"As you can see, I am very much alive," Griffin replied in an arrogant baritone buzz that sent the duke's heart into palpitations.

"Yes, but we thought you was dead. For five years now."

As Griffin looked from Dunsmore to Myra, his frown deepened. He saw no joy in his beloved's

18

eyes, but rather a cringing fear. He noticed that Myra clung to the duke as to a lifeline, and soon his sharp eyes discerned the sparkle of a large diamond on her third finger. It was not his simple band of baguettes she had been wearing when he left.

"I see," he said in a voice that would strike fear into the heart of a Norse warrior. His wicked black eyes steamed a threat in the duke's direction.

"You were gone five years, Griffin!" Myra said in a quavering voice.

"I believe seven years is the usual interval before a man is assumed dead," Griffin said.

"But you never wrote."

"The postal service was sadly irregular in the jungle," he said satirically. Myra sagged onto a sofa, and Griffin turned a steely eye on her escort. "This presents a little problem, does it not, Dunsmore?"

"We are to be married next month," the duke said weakly. "That is, we were to be . . ."

"On the twenty-first of June, Mama's wedding anniversary," Myra added.

"I see." Griffin poured wine from the tray Lady Calmet had had delivered, and passed it to the others as his mind raced over this new state of affairs. His first instinct was to laugh; his second to box Dunsmore's ears and chuck him out the door by the nape of his neck. But when he saw Myra gazing lovingly at her duke, he had to reconsider. "That leaves me three weeks to change your mind," he said.

Dunsmore was goaded into speech by this threat. "I say, old chap!"

"Come now, Dunsmore," Griffin chided. "You stole Myra while I was away. My proposition is more fair. You and I will both be here, with equal

19

opportunity to press our suit forward. I believe that is the civilized course to follow." His flashing eyes suggested other less civilized alternatives. "Or would you, like myself, prefer a swifter solution?" he asked in a voice of silken menace.

"No, no. There is no need for swiftness. We are both gentlemen, I hope."

Griffin went to Myra, and cupped her cheek in the palm of his hand. She looked up and met his searching gaze. When his lips lifted in a tender smile, she felt something strange happen inside her, something warm and tumultuous. She did not answer his smile, but she did not twitch away from his touch. Her emotions were in awful turmoil. She had always felt helpless at Griffin's touch, yet she loved Dunsmore to distraction.

It galled Dunsmore to see another man's hand on his fiancée. He wanted to object, but there was something in Griffin's sloe-berry eyes that robbed the duke of courage. He thought of that long spear, and of his unpleasant experience in Manton's shooting gallery, and knew he dare not issue a challenge, nor even object to Griffin's touching Myra. "It is really up to Myra, is it not?" he said.

They both looked at her. She felt betrayed by Dunsmore. He ought to have protected her. She took very little pleasure in the thought of being alone with Griffin, yet she was not totally averse to being the cynosure of all eyes. And with the two most desirable parties in all of Britain trailing at her skirts, she would surely be that. Her taste for admiration reveled in the prospect.

"But I am engaged to Dunsmore, Griffin," she said archly.

"You are also engaged to me," he pointed out. "Unless you are planning to give me my congé without allowing me to try to regain your love."

20

The hurt look he cast on her robbed him of menace. He really was awfully handsome.

Myra saw the spasm of alarm that seized Dunsmore, and knew that he was in agony. Served him right! He should have stood up to Griffin. "That seems fair," she said to her more recent fiancé.

Dunsmore, frightened into meaningless cliché, said, "Fair's fair."

"Then it is my turn to try my hand at regaining my fiancée's favor," Griffin said, and took Myra by the hand to help her up from the chair. They went arm in arm to the ballroom, where Myra Newbold had almost more attention than she wanted. Every eye, bright with unsatisfied curiosity, was on her. The gossip roiled around her, like gigantic waves in an ocean storm. There had never been such an interesting party since Lady Caroline Lamb took the carving knife to Lord Byron at Lady Heathcote's party. Or perhaps the knife had been aimed at herself. Reports were various as to the intended victim.

The waltzes were finished, and it was to a sedate cotillion that Lord Griffin led his fiancée, where they both performed with exquisite grace, but very little conversation. When the set was finished, Griffin led Myra to her mama. The young lady with her was quite obviously Alice, all grown up and looking quite fetching.

"Mrs. Newbold, I have come back, like the bad penny I am," Griffin said with a bow.

"I noticed," she said glumly.

"And Miss Alice," he continued. "May I have the pleasure of the next set?"

"I would like it of all things, Griffin," she smiled, and went off with him, as one in a dream.

Chapter Three

Before they had taken two steps, Lady Calmet rushed up to them, trailing her nubile daughter in her wake. The hostess doubted that Myra Newbold would exchange her ducal parti for Griffin, which left the dashing Griffin free for some other fortunate lady. Why not her own Sara?

"No fair, Miss Alice," the hostess said playfully. "You Newbolds are monopolizing Griffin. The rest of the world is also eager to hear his South American tales. Sara, dear, you remember Lord Griffin? If you ask him very nicely, perhaps he will stand up with you for the next set."

"But he asked me!" Alice objected.

As Griffin had entered without an invitation, he felt obliged to humor his hostess. He lowered his brow and said to Alice, "Later, brat." Lady Calmet's blink of surprise alerted him that he had used the old pet name. "Alice was still a child when I left," he explained. "She used to be called brat at home. I see she is scowling at me for remembering it. It just slipped out, Sal. Sorry."

"No one called me that except you," she muttered, and cast a look of loathing on Lady Sara.

"They grow up so quickly," Lady Calmet smiled. "I can scarcely believe my little Sara is such a fine young lady. I wager you scarcely recognize her, though you two were friends once." She prodded her daughter forward for approval.

Griffin remembered her very well, and could not observe much difference from the perfectly mature lady he had left five years before. She had been a striking beauty then, and she still was. The first sheen of youth had been replaced with a gloss of town bronze that was equally attractive to him. She was a statuesque brunet with black hair, green eyes, and a warm smile. "Don't be ridiculous, Mama," Lady Sara laughed. "I hope I have not deteriorated to the point where Griffin does not recognize me."

Her mother's eyes snapped. "Foolish girl!" she chided.

"It does not take a mathematician to realize I was out before Griffin left, Mama," Sara said, exchanging a smile with Griffin. "He knows how long I have hung on the vine. It is wonderful to see you again, Griffin."

"Maturity becomes you, Sara. You are as lovely as ever," he replied, and lifted her fingers to his lips.

"I see you have kept your silver tongue," Sara smiled. "And added a touch of gold to your ear."

"The better to hear you."

"Is there some particular significance to it?" she asked.

"A *mameluco* woman did it for me. It was a sort of token that I was friendly, to allow me to pass through certain hostile terrain. I shan't bore you with the story."

"But it sounds fascinating! What is this *mameluco* you mention?"

"The *mamelucos* are the result of intermarriage, usually a Portuguese father and an Indian mother."

While Griffin explained this to Sara, Lady Calmet took Alice's arm and hustled her off to another gentleman. Alice tried to console herself that she would have the next set with Griffin, but it was nothing of the sort. The ladies were on him like hounds on a fox. He was invited to call on everyone who managed a word with him. They were all suddenly fascinated by Brazil, and wished to discuss it with him over dinner, or a drive, or preferably tête-à-tête at home.

It was perfectly clear to Alice that Griffin had become the Season's lion. When she complained of Lady Calmet's stunt to Myra, it was also clear to Myra. She felt a gloating swell of satisfaction to hold Griffin's future in the palm of her dainty white hand. She could have him for the snapping of her fingers. How all these ladies would hate it! But then one of them would inevitably nab Dunny if she gave him his congé . . .

The matter required some deep thinking, but she did make one decision. She would allow Griffin to call as often as he wished during the next three weeks. He was not so frightening as she had feared. She would allow him to take her out for drives, and she would stand up with him at all the balls. And if he succeeded in winning her back— well, Dunny had agreed to give Griffin a chance, so he could not complain.

When Alice saw the ladies throwing themselves at Griffin, she knew she hadn't a chance in the world with him, even if Myra turned him off. He had practically promised he would have the next set with her, but he could not escape the throng. It was disgusting to see them all making fools of themselves. How Griffin must be laughing behind their backs—except that he was probably flattered to death. She knew instinctively that her chances would be better in the country. If she could lure Griffin to Mersham, and get Mama to go back to Newbold Hall, she might yet win him.

As Griffin had not learned the waltz, the next set of waltzes was postponed. In their stead, Griffin showed the ladies how to perform a tribal dance picked up from the Tabajo Indians. Since the orchestra did not know this alien music, Griffin chanted out the tune, and soon the most sophisticated set of adults in England were running around in circles, lifting their knees high and uttering sounds not usually heard outside of a children's school yard.

It was nearly time for the midnight dinner. Myra had said Griffin was going to join her and Dunny for dinner, and Alice meant to sit with them. There was just one more set, then dinner. Looking toward the dance floor, she saw Griffin shaking his head and laughing, as Miss Sutton tried to entice him to have the waltz with her. Of course, Griffin did not know how to waltz. The dance had not been in fashion when he left. He would sit this set out! Alice lurked around the edge of the floor, and when he escaped, she was waiting for him.

"Help!" he said. "Where can I hide? I am being hunted by a party of crazed lady waltzers."

"Follow me." Alice scooted down the hallway. Her plan was to stay in the library with Griffin until dinnertime. It was occupied by a few elderly couples who neither danced nor enjoyed cards. "We should be safe here," she said.

"You underestimate the huntresses. Miss Sutton has already suggested I join her in the library, as I

25

do not waltz." He saw a door at the end of the hall and asked where it led.

"Out to a little garden."

"Excellent. I shall be back for dinner. We still have not had our dance, Alice. There is something I most particularly want to discuss with you."

"Me?" she asked, flattered.

"You are the only one who can help me."

Her heart took flight, and her foolish imagination soared to unimagined heights. He realized he did not love Myra. All the huntresses had given him a disgust of beautiful ladies. In short, he loved her, and wished to make a declaration.

"I'll go with you now," she said promptly.

"Leave the ball with a gent? Aren't you the racy thing, you young limb of the devil."

"We are old friends. You are practically my brother-in-law," she said, peering for his reaction.

He considered this a moment, then said, "Let us go then, before someone sees us."

They went down the hall and out the door into a small garden, enclosed by yews. The nominal garden consisted of a cement apron holding two stone flowerpots and flanked by one laurel tree. There was an uncomfortable stone bench and a small table. The night was still and pleasantly fresh after the turmoil of the ballroom. A pearly white moon floated in the black void of space, surrounded by a sprinkle of diamond stars.

"How can I help you, Griffin?" she asked in a voice trying to sound romantic.

"Do you have a cold, brat? Your voice sounds hoarse. Perhaps we should go back inside."

"I am fine," she said curtly.

Griffin stood with his hands behind his back, gazing up at the moon. "Tell me about her," he said. "I mean about her and Dunsmore. She cannot love him."

Alice's soaring hopes plunged to earth and crashed. She sunk onto the edge of the stone bench. Her. He had not even used Myra's name. There was only one woman where Griffin was concerned. Alice damped down the urge to tell him Myra was not good enough for him. She only wanted a life of ease and privilege. She lacked the daring to go off to Brazil. But really he must know what she was like, in his deepest heart. He knew it, and he still loved her. Alice would do as she always did; she would tell him the truth.

"I think she does love him. People say he is quite clever, you know, about the Corn Laws and things."

"He keeps his cleverness on a tight rein. I saw no sign of it."

"He's afraid of you." Griffin smiled. "I never said he was brave. He's sensitive. Myra likes that in a man. You were gone five years, Griffin. She used to talk about you all the time at first, and spend hours writing letters. But when years went by without an answer . . ."

"I didn't get those letters. I answered all the ones I received. It was impossible to communicate from the Amazon. I thought she would realize that."

"But five years!"

"What's past is prologue. Does she not love me at all? Has she forgotten all we meant to each other? I cannot believe it."

She heard the pain beneath the words. His bronzed face looked pale in the moonlight. Pale, and vulnerable. If Alice could have waved a magic wand, she would have made Myra love him. "She thought you were dead, Griffin. Now that you are back, maybe you can make her love you again," she said in a small voice.

"I must!" he said, his jaw firming. "And you must help me, Alice. You are her sister, closer to her than anyone. What can I do to make her love me as she did before?"

"She does not like anything too—different," she said, not satisfied with the vague word. Griffin's hand went to his earring. "Not that. That is rather picaresque. I daresay it will set a new fad. At least I heard a few bucks wondering where they could get one. I meant she was terrified when Mr. Barnaby said your face was black and you were carrying a spear, and someone mentioned an orangutan."

"Ignoramuses. There are no orangutans in Brazil. It was a harmless little monkey." He shook his head, smiling ruefully. "I knew this dark skin would be my undoing. It will fade eventually, but meanwhile I cannot bleach it. What can I do?"

"She loved you once. Behave as you did before. Don't frighten her. Don't talk loud or argue. Myra likes to be comfortable."

"Yes, her gentle disposition never could tolerate any wrangling. I have brought back an incredibly beautiful orchid. It is pure white, with a blush of pink at the heart. A rare and lovely thing. I thought of her when I first espied it. I mean to cultivate it and call it after her."

Alice felt a wicked stab of jealousy. "She'll like that," she said. "That sort of thing pleases her. Flowers and poetry—sensitive things."

"I am no poet, but I hope I am sensitive as Dunsmore."

"The orchid will do as well. He isn't really sensitive, just squeamish."

"I shall tread softly, as you suggest. I daresay that means I must not call Dunsmore out. Pity. That would be the easiest solution."

"You must not even *think* such a thing, Griffin."

"I was teasing, brat," he laughed.

"I wish you would not call me that. I am all grown up now."

"And a fine job you and Mother Nature have done of it. I am impressed," he said, but she knew by his voice it was mere duty speaking.

"Does Dunsmore write her poems?" he asked.

"No, they read poems together. Mostly she reads, and he praises her."

"I can listen and praise," he said, frowning at such a lackluster way of winning a bride. "What I should like to do is write up my Brazilian experiences for the journals and dedicate them to Myra. I have made copious notes and drawings for articles for the scientific societies, but I think something of a more general nature for the public at large might go off well, too. A book of essay, perhaps."

"She would like that."

When he did not reply, Alice sensed he was ready to speak of other things now, and she was curious to hear about his adventures. "What was it like in Brazil, Griffin? Did you really see pygmies?"

"See them? I lived with them. You cannot possibly imagine what it is like there, Alice. I have had such incredible adventures, no one would believe the half of them. I have plowed through steaming jungles, and killed wild boar with a spear."

"Did you kill lions and tigers?"

"There is no large game in Brazil—well, the tapir, a sort of cross between a wild boar and a rhinoceros. I saw one in the *selva*, but it got away. I have dined in Rio with Dom John and his court, off silver plates, and eaten alligator with my fingers around a fire with two dozen native Indians who spoke not a word of either English or Portuguese. I have watched *macumba* at work—there is a book in itself."

"What is *macumba*?"

"Black magic, I suppose you would call it. An African religion. They call it *candomblé* in Bahia, where it is particularly rife. I have dug for diamonds—"

"Did you bring home a trunkful? Someone said so."

"No, I had no luck, but I bought a few before leaving Rio de Janeiro. I plan to have the finest one made into a ring for Myra."

"That sounds lovely," Alice said dutifully. "What other experiences have you had, Griffin?"

"I was bitten by some insect and got a terrible infection shortly after I left Rio. It happened on board ship on the Parana River. The infection was debilitating, and you can imagine the sort of medical help there was available. I was literally at death's door. I thought I would never see her again."

"Tell her that—but don't talk too much about the infection. Just say you were at death's door, and all you could think was that you would never see her again."

"That was not all I thought. I also thought that Monty would take over Mersham, as he has. I must make a dart home and take care of that. I have had my man of business write him that I am back."

"You will be going home soon then?" she asked eagerly.

"For a quick visit, yes. I dare not leave Myra alone with Dunsmore. Why did she choose *him*? Other than being a duke, he hasn't much to offer. Or do the ladies see something that I do not?"

"Oh, he is all right," Alice said, searching in vain for one real attribute to bolster her claim. "He is

30

very considerate," she said, after a moment's pause. "How did you get cured of your infection? Did you not take basilicum and things with you?"

"I did, but my medicine trunk got thrown overboard in a storm. It hardly mattered. The medications proved ineffectual with the strange new diseases there. It was a primitive medicine man who saved my life with some native herbs. I was too weak to walk for months."

"You should have come home as soon as you could walk," she said.

"Perhaps I should have, but the plant life there! It was astonishing. I brought back wagon loads of specimens. I am sharing them with the botanists in London. I am also eager to get to Mersham and begin cultivating them."

"When will you be going home?"

"That depends on my luck in detaching my fiancée from Dunsmore," he said. "And now I shall take you in, or I shall have your mama accusing me of depraving her daughter." His laughing voice said more clearly than words that such a thing had never entered his mind.

They returned, and soon it was time for dinner. Myra was heady with pride at the attention she received as she sat with the two prime parties of the Season flanking her. She doled out her conversation equally to the gentleman on either side, and graciously agreed that as she was engaged to them both, she could have a second dance with both after dinner without offending the proprieties. Alice did not have her dance with Griffin after all, but she did receive one crumb of consolation.

Before they left he said, "Do you know this lascivious new waltz that is all the craze, Sal?"

"Of course. I have had permission from the patronesses of Almack's to do it. Do you take me for a flat?"

"Not you! Will you teach me how to do it?"

She was delighted at the opportunity to be alone with him, but had to wonder why he did not ask Myra to teach him. When she put the question to him, he replied, "I am afraid I would walk all over her."

"But you don't mind walking all over me!"

"I shall buy you a bag of sugarplums," he said, smiling to cover his embarrassment.

"I am not a child, Griffin!"

"But you'll teach me the waltz?"

"Very well, but it cannot be done in any hole-in-the-wall fashion. You must come to the house, and Mama or someone will play the pianoforte for us."

"We'll settle some hour when Dunsmore is being given his opportunity to solidify his position vis-à-vis my fiancée," he said, with a satirical curl of the lip.

"And *his* fiancée. Fancy Myra having two beaux."

"And poor you has not even nabbed one. You are slow off the mark, Sal."

"I had offers!"

"They cannot have been good ones, or you would be bounced off by now."

"They were excellent offers!"

"Then why did you not accept?"

She bit her lip in frustration. Griffin was not interested enough to pursue the matter, but he did think of it, among other things, as he drove home. Little Alice, all grown up and trying to act like a lady, and some gents actually thinking she would make a suitable bride. It made him realize how long he had been away, and the changes that had occurred during that time. But mostly he thought of Myra, who seemed even more alluring, as she was now a prize that must be competed for. He would win her back yet. He had not crossed jungles and oceans, only to be outdone by that simpering idiot, Dunsmore.

Chapter Four

With the best intentions in the world, Lord Griffin was not able to lavish the attention on his fiancée that he had wished to, and that he had felt the situation demanded. The world had discovered him, and it seemed that a large part of the world came to Grosvenor Square to pay him court. Every journal worth its salt sent reporters to interview his lordship. Every scholarly society and every social club was eager for him to join their numbers. Society hostesses too vied for his presence at their soirees. London had not seen such lionizing since Lord Byron published his *Cantoes*, and awoke one morning to find himself famous.

Jewelers did a flourishing business in small golden hoops for gentlemen's ears. When Griffin dashed out in a downpour one morning in a pair of old gaucho boots to save his new Hessians, the boot makers were besieged by requests for these strange-looking articles, of a soft leather that hung loosely about the ankles, like a pair of hose several sizes too large. The sedate paisley shawl, beloved by ladies of fashion, was replaced by hand-loomed shawls of exotic flowered prints. Griffin had brought home some lengths of Indian textile, and gave them to a few callers. It was Lady Sara who had the inspiration of adding a fringe and turning hers into a shawl. If it came from Griffin, it had to be stunning. He had become the very glass of fashion and mold of form.

The Duke of Devonshire said frankly that Brummell in his heyday could not fasten Griffin's shoe buckle when it came to style. Word of Griffin's fame spread to Brighton, and the prince had himself hoisted into his carriage and driven to London to meet the new Adonis. But first he took half a dozen sunbaths to tint his sluggish complexion.

A piquancy was added to the whole by the triangular arrangement of Griffin's engagement to Miss Newbold, who was simultaneously betrothed to the illustrious Duke of Dunsmore. Which would she choose? The advantages of the ducal parti—his fortune and his various estates—were too well-known to require enumeration. Of course Dunny was a bit of a fool, but a good chap withal. Griffin, on the other hand, was also noble, and while not so disgustingly rich, how many houses could one lady live in? Griffin was so very handsome, so gallant, so manly.

It was felt that Lady Jersey summed it up aptly when she said: "It all depends on whether Miss Newbold marries with her heart or her head." The odds at the younger gentlemen's clubs ran in favor of heart; at the sanctuaries of the elderly, Dunsmore had the edge. No bets were placed among the ladies; they agreed unanimously that she would choose Griffin.

Miss Newbold herself was in a fever of indecision. She loved Dunsmore dearly, and suffered along with him the pangs of her vacillation. But then when Griffin came sweeping into her mama's saloon, bringing with him trinkets and stories from the wilds of South America, and a whiff of notoriety (for he was not so discreet as a fiancée could wish regarding his interviews with the press), she felt she would be mad not to choose him.

The notoriety involved, among other things, a certain Indian princess called Nwani, who had been given to Griffin by her papa for some brave escapade during the wild boar hunt. Griffin was quoted as having said it would be a fatal insult to refuse her. The princess had not returned with him to England, but as no fatality had befallen him, Myra was inclined to think he had accepted the lady at least temporarily.

This, however, did not prevent her from dashing through Hyde Park in his newly acquired curricle, with an albino monkey called Snow White riding bobbin on the front of the carriage. This mischievous creature actually terrified Myra. Snow White was fiercely jealous of her master, and struck out at any lady who got too close to him. She had actually tried to bite Myra, who was fortunately wearing kid gloves at the time, which was all that had prevented the sharp teeth from penetrating her flesh.

Myra liked the *idea* of being in Griffin's company, but when she was actually with him, she was invariably in a state of agitation that prevented her from enjoying it. He had removed the more objectionable external traces of the savage from his toilette, but she sensed a lurking primitivism beneath the bronze skin and golden earring. Even his compliments were savage.

"Why is that fellow smirking at you? I'll darken the cawker's daylights if he doesn't stop," he had said the other day on Bond Street. "I don't want anyone but me looking at you like that. All your own fault for being so beautiful." Surely he should not have blamed a lady for the misbehavior of a perfect stranger? She could not help being so beautiful.

The sensible alternative of seeking privacy with Griffin never occurred to her. She claimed to love her privacy, but one could only conclude that she loved it platonically. She went about complaining of crowds and attention wherever she could find them. Bond Street, Hyde Park, balls, and routs were their usual destinations.

To add another arrow to his quiver, Griffin stuck to his intention of learning the waltz. He managed to squeeze two morning waltz lessons with Alice into his tempestuous schedule. These occurred while Dunsmore was having his chance with his fiancée. Mrs. Newbold was marble constant in her choice of the duke as a son-in-law. She was much too busy to indulge her younger daughter by playing the piano for her, but she was glad to keep Griffin away from Myra and arranged for a friend to do the job. They were to be private lessons, just the one couple and Mrs. Chambers to act as pianist cum chaperon.

"It is really very simply once you get the hang of it," Alice explained. "The count is three. Right foot forward, left foot forward, right foot joins the left." But when they tried it, they waltzed smartly into each other.

"You have to dance backward, Griffin."

"Good God! It is difficult enough trying to do it forward."

It was not made any easier, in Alice's view, by the fact that Griffin held her so tightly in his arms. Unaware of the fine points of waltzing etiquette, he crushed her firmly against his broad chest, with their bodies touching intimately from shoulder to knee. She was in no hurry to enlighten him as to the proper distance. When he began to get the hang of it, he relaxed and enjoyed it.

His head inclined to hers and his dark eyes gleamed mischievously. "I could get to like this. Do you think society is going to hell in a hand basket? Nothing like this delightful debauchery was permitted when I left England."

The chaperon cleared her throat in a meaningful way, and Alice said, "Actually you are holding me too tightly, Griffin. Our bodies are not supposed to touch. The chaperons say they should be able to see two inches of air between us."

"I knew there would be a catch to it," he laughed. "They could see more than air between a couple dancing like this, if they kept their eyes open. This teasing dance has to be a French invention."

As Griffin made no move to loosen his arms, Alice stepped back the necessary two inches. "The waltz comes from Austria, actually."

"That surprises me. The Germans usually take their music so seriously. Sorry," he said, as he stepped on her toe.

"Maybe you should just be quiet and count, Griffin," she suggested.

Being quiet was virtually impossible for this inveterate chatterbox. "I am making strides with Myra," he said.

"She was pleased with that lace mantle from Portugal, but I suggest you leave Snow White home the next time you drive with her."

"Pity. It was Snow White who catapulted her into my arms at the park. We went for a stroll. Snow White tried to disengage Myra's hand from mine. She shouted—Myra, that is, and flew to my arms to be rescued. I kissed her."

"In the park, in broad daylight?" She missed a beat and walked on his toe.

"Just a small kiss. She did not object. Sorry."

"That was my fault. So she let you kiss her?" This seemed an evil harbinger. Myra was nice to a fault. If she was letting Griffin kiss her, she must have made up her mind to have him.

"Yes, and tonight, I plan to increase the pressure."

"What is happening tonight? We are attending the theater. Oh, Griffin, you are not going to do something foolish like address her from the stage? Truly, I do not think she would like that. It sounds vulgar—though it sounds very romantic, too," she added wistfully.

"Don't be a goosecap. Of course I am not going to embarrass her publicly. No, I have a different surprise."

"Tell me. I shan't tell anyone."

"You have no notion of discretion," he said thoughtlessly.

Alice took this charge amiss. Was she not hiding the greatest secret of her life in her bosom? Griffin had no suspicion that she was madly in love with him. He treated her like a friend, and she did not betray by so much of a flicker of an eyelash that her heart was breaking.

"I won't tell. I promise."

"Very well then, but remember, you promised. We are not attending the theater after all. I have been invited to a different party, and plan to take Myra with me. Dunsmore is not invited," he added, and laughed.

"Then she won't go."

"I think she will. It is more or less a command

performance, you see. The Prince of Wales has invited me to Carlton House. He has arranged a small soiree especially in my honor. Only the crème de la crème will be there. You and your mama are also invited, by the by."

"Really!" she exclaimed, eyes wide. "Oh, Griffin, we have never been there. She will love it of all things. And you have not told Myra?"

"No, I mean to surprise her. I shall pretend we are going to the theater, then switch course and deliver her to Carlton House. I feel I ought to hire white chargers for the occasion."

"Drive whatever you like, but tell Myra where she is going. She will want to make a special toilette."

"Myra is always dressed to the nines. I want to surprise her. Don't spoil my surprise, brat."

"But really, I don't think—"

"You promised."

The waltz ended and as the hour was up, they thanked Mrs. Chambers and took her to join Mrs. Newbold for tea, then returned to the music room to put away the music.

"I think you are making a mistake not to tell her," Alice said.

Griffin was not the sort of gentleman to be plagued by self-doubts. "No, I'm not. I know Myra as well as you do. Can you keep another secret?"

"Yes."

Griffin reached inside his jacket and drew out a small box. He flipped the lid, revealing a very large round diamond, set in gold. Sunlight struck the facets, sending off a myriad of tiny, intensely colored rainbows. Red and purple, green and orange shimmered in the sunlight.

"It is beautiful, Griffin! And so big!"

"Try it on. I want to see how it looks on," he said, and took it up to put on her finger.

As their hands fumbled together, Alice had to bite her lips to keep from moaning. She felt tears rush to her eyes, for she was overcome by the symbolic meaning of the gesture. If only it was really meant for her.

"Do you think she'll like it?" He held her hand, twisting it this way and that, to catch the light.

His hand felt warm and strong as it held hers. Alice was overcome with a swelling of grief that nearly killed her. "How could she not? I never saw anything so beautiful in my life," she sighed.

"It is a beauty, is it not? A flawless stone. It is called a blue diamond, although it is not really blue. It is ten carats. I saw the thing Dunsmore gave her. Not more than five, and the setting is ugly."

"It belonged to his grandmama." She reluctantly pulled the ring off and handed it to him. "You don't feel you are rushing her, Griffin? She has not said anything to indicate that she is ready to make up her mind."

"She let me kiss her. Damme, she's had a week. How long does she plan to lead the two of us about on a leash? I don't know about Dunsmore, but I am getting demmed tired of it."

This was the first chink in the armor of his love, and Alice heard it with renewed hope. But she would not say a word to widen the chink. "It is hard for her. I daresay she does not want to hurt Dunsmore's feelings. He is—"

"I know. Sensitive." Griffin frowned, trying to reconcile himself to Myra's dawdling ways. "A week should be long enough," he said.

"What will you do if she says no?"

41

"I shall go to Mersham, as I ought to have done a week ago. I have heard from Monty."

"What did he say?" she asked. "I expect he was very upset. Poor Monty. One has to feel sorry for him, losing out on his expectations."

"I have no doubt he was devastated, but you would never know it from the letter he sent, congratulating me, and expressing delight at my safe deliverance. It makes me fear he has savaged the estate."

"Oh no, he is a wonderful manager, Griffin. Better than—that is, Mersham has never been in better shape."

He lifted a black brow. "Do I sense a little disapproval in there, brat? You disapprove of my wandering ways?"

"A man should be at home to look after his estate, especially when he has such a valuable one as Mersham."

"Fear not. I plan to settle down. I have promised Myra I shan't peel off to South America again." His voice held just a hint of resentment.

Alice felt an instinctive urge to console him, and reached for his fingers. "You have had one excellent adventure anyway, Griffin. That is more than most people. The only exciting things that ever happened to me were measles and a broken collarbone when I fell off my mount." When she realized what she was doing, she shyly withdrew her hand.

Griffin patted it unthinkingly. "You are young, Sal. Your turn for excitement will come. Mine is past." She looked at him, frowning. "You misunderstand me. I am ready to settle down with Myra. That will be excitement enough for me."

They stood a moment in silence, pondering this thought, both in their different ways, then Griffin said, "I had best be leaving. I have half a dozen gentlemen calling this afternoon. I shall be here at eight this evening. You'll make sure your mama and Myra are ready? One cannot be late for Carlton House."

"Of course not, but don't expect the prince to be punctual. What should we wear?"

"The finest rags and jewels you possess. No danger of outshining Prinny. His costumes would put fireworks to shame. But remember, don't tell the others my surprise." He bowed, said, "*Atea logo,*" and left. He often threw in these foreign phrases. Alice found them charming, even if she didn't know what they meant.

She sat on alone in the music room, thinking over the visit. She was angry at Myra's insisting that Griffin not travel anymore. He agreed to it now, to win her, but she was by no means sure he could stick to it. Nor was she sure Myra had the right to demand it of him. Collecting rare specimens was his work, as the Corn Laws were Dunsmore's. If she loved him, she would not set these conditions. The trouble was, Griffin didn't understand Myra. She was just a homebody, whose head was turned with all the attention she was receiving.

Dunsmore had seemed the perfect match for her. Oh, why had Griffin not delayed his return by another month, and everything would have been all right. This "surprise" was a wretched idea. Myra didn't like surprises. She never wore her best gowns to the theater to get crushed by an evening of sitting. She would end up at Carlton House in a second-best gown, and be furious. Perhaps the diamond ring would smooth her ruffled feathers. Alice relived that moment when Griffin had put it on her finger.

Then she went to her room to sort through her

gowns and choose the best one for that evening. Tonight would settle it one way or the other. Myra would either accept the ring and turn Dunsmore off, or she would refuse it and turn Griffin off. Alice was on thorns, wondering what would be the outcome.

If Myra turned him off, he would return to Mersham. She would soon return to Newbold Hall, right next door. Griffin would need someone to solace him in his sorrow, and she would be there . . .

Chapter Five

"You are not wearing that gown!" Alice exclaimed, when Myra appeared for dinner in one of her less elegant creations. It was another ice-blue gown, her favorite color, to match her eyes.

"It is comfortable," Myra said. "I shall wear my paisley shawl over it."

"And those pearls?" Alice said, thinking of the diamond necklace that would at least add a touch of glitter to the ensemble.

"Good gracious, Alice, we are only going to the theater. One would think we were going to Carlton House, the way you speak."

A strangled sigh caught in Alice's throat as she bit back the secret.

When Griffin called for them, he noticed nothing amiss with Myra's toilette. "Charming," he said, bowing to his beloved, and tossing an inclusive smile to the other ladies.

"We shall meet Dunsmore at the theater," Myra said. "It was kind of him to give us his box. He and his cousin will use the other seats."

This theater party was Myra's doing. She thought she might find it easier to make up her mind if she had her two fiancés together, side by side, for an evening. Usually she went out with them one at a time. Dunsmore had not been happy with her scheme, but she could always bring him 'round her thumb. Griffin, on the other hand, seemed to relish any chance to be in the same room with Dunsmore, and pester the poor soul.

No treachery was suspected as Griffin's carriage wheeled past Piccadilly. The left turn on to Pall Mall was still heading toward the theater. It had to slow down at the row of Ionic columns and round arch of Carlton House as there was a gathering of carriages there awaiting entry.

"I hope we are not going to be late," Myra said.

"I doubt the party will get underway without us," Griffin replied.

"Don't be silly, Griffin. They will not hold the curtain for us," Myra laughed.

When the driver wheeled in at the round arch of Carlton House, Mrs. Newbold let out a shout. "No really, Griffin! You go too far! One is not allowed to drive around within the prince's private estate, although I should love to see the gardens. There is no saying he might not be out taking the air, and he hates being stared at. Small wonder. He has grown to elephantine proportions."

"I shall ask the prince to give you a tour," Griffin said.

"Oh, this is horrid!" Myra squealed. "We shall be locked in the tower. Do make your coachman turn around, Griffin. And besides, we shall be late for the play."

"We are not going to the theater," he said, with the air of one conferring a great treat. "We are invited to Carlton House."

46

"Carlton House!" Myra gasped. "Don't be absurd. I cannot go to Carlton House. I am not even wearing my diamonds."

"You are a diamond of the first water. What need have you of lesser stones?"

"I am wearing my blue gown," she said, her voice rising shrilly.

"I noticed it in particular. It is charming."

Mrs. Newbold, while not loath to get a toe into Carlton House, was beside herself with chagrin at not knowing beforehand, and being prepared. "You might have told us, Griffin. I would have had my hair done. One never dresses up for the theater. I don't know what the prince will think."

"I told you so!" Alice said angrily to Griffin.

Mrs. Newbold turned a beady eye on her younger daughter. "You never mean you knew all the while and did not give us a word of warning! Upon my word, I have been harboring a viper in my bosom."

Other concerns had occurred to Myra. "What about Dunsmore? He will be wondering what has happened to me."

"I sent him a note. He should be receiving it about now," Griffin said. He was disappointed that his treat had failed to please. At Myra's next question, his disappointment rose to vexation. There was no pleasing the wench.

"Will he be joining us here?" she asked.

"No, he is not invited," he said curtly.

"We shall leave early and meet him after the play," Myra announced, to repay him for his sharp tone.

"Goose!" her mama said. "One cannot leave a party until the prince leaves." Carlton House hove into view through the carriage window, and she was distracted by it. "I call that shabby," she said.

"It is all covered in filth and grime. Why does he not give it a coat of lime wash?"

As her wandering eye espied the lavish use of torches and royal footmen in their dark blue livery festooned with gold lace, her spirits rose. No doubt it would be better inside.

And indeed it was. It was a regular Versailles, so far as gilt and trim went. When the prince, all aglitter in white satin, his medals a tinkle, bowed over her hand, the last of her annoyance faded, to be replaced by unadulterated bliss. The prince was as fat as everyone said, but it was every ounce royal fat, and full of breeding. Even the squeaking of his corsets had a regal sound.

"Mrs. Newbold," the prince said. "And these would be your charming daughters, of whom one hears so much."

Myra and Alice performed stiff curtsies, and both had the distinction of being proclaimed incomparables. It was His Majesty's unimaginative compliment to any lady too young to interest his jaded taste.

It was soon clear where the prince's true interest lay. He got Griffin by the elbow and led him off to display him like a trophy, before steering him to a private office for a good coze. "About this Princess Nwani, Griffin. A bit of a goer, was she? Is it true the ladies go about naked to the waist?"

Prinny's departure left Mrs. Newbold free to take an inventory of the gold and glitter hiding behind the smoked facade of Carlton House.

It was well-known among the prince's *intimes* that he held himself responsible for winning the Battle of Waterloo, and before the evening was over, he also assumed credit for having discovered Brazil. He quizzed Griffin on his adventures, and urged him to write the whole up in a book for posterity. "We will be proud to have it dedicated to us," he said with a bow.

The ladies were not entirely abandoned. The prince handed them over to his bosom beau, the Countess de Lieven. This lively shrew was married to the Russian ambassador. The countess collared Mr. DeSouza, the Portuguese ambassador, and the ugliest man in Christendom, to entertain Mrs. Newbold with his salacious stories. The provincials liked to be shocked. The younger girls were taken to the ballroom, and partners were found for them. There was dancing, and at eleven o'clock, dinner was served. No turtle soup, quails, or capons graced the table. The guests fed on cold cuts and custard. The prince was once again on a diet. At eleven-thirty, the prince retired, and the guests were free to go or stay, as they pleased.

Griffin suggested they leave. He planned to top off the evening with a champagne party at the Pulteny Hotel. It was on the wave of royal favor, crested with lavish servings of champagne, that he meant to present the diamond ring and win Myra once and for all. Myra hoped they would meet Dunsmore there, and agreed to go to the hotel. She was eager to frighten the duke with the wonderful evening Griffin had arranged.

Griffin was forgiven for having surprised her. The prince had called her incomparable, and really there had not been any other young gentlemen there who would have appreciated her more elegant toilettes. In fact, she modestly admitted that outside of the prince himself, she was the most elegant creature in the room. The Countess de Lieven wore an ugly old puce turban, without even a feather in it.

Alice was usually the first lady into her pelisse.

She joined Griffin, who was waiting near the door, smiling triumphantly.

"Was I right, or was I right, brat?" he asked.

"She would have liked it better if you had let her know in advance."

"Very likely, but *I* would not have liked it half as well. She would have pouted me into inviting Dunsmore. You were alerted. How does it come you are not decked in diamonds and finery?"

"This is my best gown! It has spangles and everything," she said, pointing to a sprinkle of spangles at the very hem of the skirt. "I don't own any diamonds," she added, hurt at his oblique charge of dowdiness.

"Sorry, Sal. You look very nice," he said, embarrassed.

"The prince said I was an incomparable. He said Myra was, too. I daresay he says that to all the young ladies. What were you and he talking about all evening, Griffin?"

"We discussed our Brazilian experiences," he replied, with one of his wicked grins. "In fact, we are thinking of writing a book about them."

"I suggest you leave out the bit about the Princess Nwani. Myra did not care for that story."

"Funny, it was Prinny's favorite."

"Did you really—you know—marry her?" she said primly.

"I did not marry her," he replied mischievously.

"But did you—the story said it would be a fatal insult to refuse her."

"You'll have to ask Prinny—or wait and buy the book," he said, looking at the blush that suffused her cheeks. In the old days, Sal would not have blushed; but then the old Sal would not have known about such wicked things as sex. He felt a stab of nostalgia that she had changed.

"I think that's horrid of you."

"Don't be an ass, Sal. I did not marry her, unless having our heads bound together with vines constitutes marriage among the Tabajo. Certainly the ceremony was not consummated. There, now are you satisfied?"

So much had changed in five years, and he had missed it all. Even Myra had changed, in some manner he could not quite put a finger on. She was still beautiful; in fact, more beautiful than before. She had matured from a shy girl into a shy lady, but no longer so shy as to give in to his every whim as she used to. It was difficult for her, having to jilt Dunsmore. He appreciated her scruples, but he was becoming demmed impatient to get on with the wedding.

"You look sad, Griffin," Alice said, watching him.

"I am not sad, exactly. It is just—they call it *saudades* in Portuguese."

"What does it mean?"

"You cannot put it into English."

"Everything can be translated into English," she said stubbornly.

"*Bruxa.*"

"I suppose that is some sort of insult."

"That one has a translation at least. It means witch. *Saudades* would take a whole essay to describe. It is a sort of nostalgia, a yearning for what is past, a kind of pleasurable sense of loss. I don't know."

Myra and Mrs. Newbold arrived, and Griffin turned his attention to ushering the ladies to the carriage. Their excited chatter filled the short journey to the hotel.

Dunsmore was not at the hotel, as Myra had hoped, but there were so many other members of the *ton* there that she was admired to her entire satisfaction. Word of Prinny's party preceded them, and the room buzzed with excitement when they entered.

Lady Sara ran over to quiz them. "Is it true you have been at Carlton House, Griffin?" she demanded, and was assured that it was. "Tell me all about it. Every word. What did he say?"

Myra blushed shyly and replied, "He said I was an incomparable. Old silly, and me in this old blue gown. Griffin was horrid! He pretended we were going to the theater, then whisked me off to Carlton House."

"What had he to say about your adventures, Griffin?" Lady Sara said, for her real interest was in the gentleman.

"He stole Griffin away from me for the whole evening," Myra replied. "But the Countess de Lieven arranged partners for me. Lord Beresford, and Sir Humphrey Dodge."

"Dunsmore was not there?" Lady Sara asked eagerly. She was not too proud to take Myra's leavings.

"I think—but you must not breathe a word—that Griffin pulled a very sly stunt on Dunny," Myra said. "He sent the duke off to the theater alone!" A rill of triumphant laughter hung on the air.

"Shabby, Griffin!" Lady Sara chided.

"I think it was a wretched thing to do," Alice said, with an accusing glare at Griffin.

"I agree," Griffin said with a bow, "but all's fair in love and war, ladies. If Dunsmore wishes to call me out, I shan't refuse the challenge. Like the Guards, I may die, but I shall not surrender." He studied Myra as he delivered this gallant threat.

She smiled her satisfaction, and went on with some more self-congratulatory nonsense, while Mrs. Newbold looked on in pique. Griffin could vulgarize even a visit to Carlton House. She disliked especially any hint at a duel. She did not care much for that sharp look in Lady Sara's eyes either. She would have the wits to snap up Dunsmore in a flash. Or Griffin for that matter. Of course, she was a regular ape-leader. She was already old news when Myra had made her bows five years ago.

Alice also looked on in disapproval at Griffin's bantering. All this attention was going to Myra's head. Could Griffin not see what a vain girl she was? "Let us have the champagne and go home," she said crossly. "My head aches from the awful lights and heat of Carlton House."

"Amen," Griffin agreed, and hailed a waiter.

Nothing meriting the name conversation occurred while they were at the Pulteny. A constant stream of friends stopped by and were told that the prince, old silly, insisted that Myra was an incomparable. Alice did not bother to add that he had also called her an imcomparable. Where was the compliment in that, when his idea of a pretty lady was the plump and aging matron, Lady Hertford?

Lord Griffin remained unaware of Myra's vanity. She was smiling on him that evening, and that was enough. He felt sure his trick had worked. He would offer her the diamond when they got home. This would require some privacy, and he managed a word with Alice to help him arrange it.

"I mean to strike while the iron is hot," he whispered, while Myra was busy with one of the guests who stopped at their table. "Can you get your mama out of the saloon on some ruse? She seems strangely averse to leaving me alone with Myra. Odd, when one considers we are engaged."

"I shall claim a headache, and call her upstairs. But I cannot promise she will remain away long, Griffin. You must work quickly."

"I always do. Thanks, brat," he said, and chucked her chin.

She tossed her head angrily. "I have asked you not to call me that, Griffin. You forget, the prince also called me an incomparable tonight."

Her eyes glittered with blocked tears. Her proud little head added a new note of dignity. Griffin studied her and said, "And he was right. You have gone and grown up on me, while my back was turned. I shan't torment you with old memories again. From now on, you are Miss Alice."

A reluctant smile drew her lips into a moue. "I don't mind if you call me Sal," she said. "It is just that brat is so degrading. I am five feet and five inches now. Taller than Myra."

"Yes, I noticed you come up to my chin," he said, bemused by this trace of the flirt in little Sal.

At last they left the Pulteny. Mrs. Newbold, in a generous mood after her exciting evening, invited Griffin in. "We shall have a cup of tea to settle our stomachs after this rare evening," she said.

Alice caught Griffin's eye and said, "I shall go up to bed, if you don't mind. I am not feeling very well, Mama."

"Run along, dear. We shan't be long."

When Alice, hanging over the banister, saw the tea tray being carried in, she ran to her room and called her mama's dresser. "Will you ask Mama to come up?" she said, holding her head. "I feel so wretched, I fear I may need the doctor."

"Mercy child, you look pink all over. Scramble into bed, and I shall send for your mama."

The message was delivered belowstairs. Myra directed a frightened glance at her mama, at being left alone with the savage.

"I shan't be a moment," Mrs. Newbold assured her, and nipped upstairs.

"At last we are alone," Griffin said, and smiled a smile that sent shivers shooting through Myra's whole body.

Chapter Six

Griffin rose and sat beside Myra on the sofa. He took her hand and lifted it to his lips. "Myra, darling, it has been a week—" he said, and smiled hopefully at her.

Myra's eyelashes fluttered chaotically. She was more than a little curious to see how Griffin's private lovemaking had changed from days of yore, yet she was also extremely uneasy.

"I know, Griffin," she said. "I have been trying to make up my mind."

His lambent, steaming eyes devoured her, and when he spoke, his voice was a silken insinuation. "Let me help you," he said, and without further ado, he drew her into his arms for a kiss that set her heart banging like a drum in her breast, and her mind reeling. Accustomed to Dunsmore's chaste embraces, she was not prepared for this sort of onslaught. She soon pushed him away.

"Well?" he said.

"I—oh, Griffin, it is so very hard, but I *think* I love you more," she said breathlessly. "At least I do not feel like this with Dunsmore." Whether she quite liked feeling "like this" was what she wished to ponder. The racing pulse and the reeling head were enjoyable for a short period, but whether she wanted to actually live with such violent sensations was a moot point.

Griffin, already sure he had carried the day, produced the diamond ring and slid it on her finger. When she was out with Griffin, she removed the ring Dunsmore had given her. The diamond felt like a deadweight on her finger. Its cold glitter overpowered her dainty hand.

"It is very large," she said, without a trace of enthusiasm, and pulled it off.

"As a symbol of my enormous love for you," he replied, shoving it back on.

She pulled it off and handed it to him. "You keep it until I have made up my mind, Griffin."

"As I said, you have had a week, Myra. In fact, we have known each other from the cradle, and you have, presumably, known Dunsmore well for longer than a week. It is time to make up your mind, my dear. You cannot keep two grown men in limbo forever. Dunsmore—or me. You must decide, now."

Myra thought of her trip to Carlton House, and of all the commotion she caused when she was on the strut with Griffin. She realized that the bronzed face and dark eyes regarding her were more handsome by far than Dunsmore's pallid features. She had even ceased finding the little gold earring strange. Yet she had truly loved Dunny. It was impossible! How could she decide? She loved them both.

Her instinctive reaction to such frustration was to cry, and she did so now. Myra cried beautifully. There was no sniffling, no red nose, but a slow blooming of crystal tears in her matchless blue eyes, accompanied by trembling lips. "I cannot decide. I love you both. Don't make me say something I shall regret, dear Griffin. Give me a little longer."

Griffin was touched by her tears, and could not demand an immediate decision. He felt like a monster, yet he was desperate to have the thing wrapped up, one way or the other. He patted her fingers, and told her not to cry. Of course she must have a little longer.

"I do not want to rush you, but you must know I have extremely urgent business at Mersham. I cannot put off going home much longer. I hoped I might carry my fiancée home with me."

Myra sensed a reprieve. With Griffin at Mersham and her and Dunny in town, she could continue her triumph as Griffin's sweetheart, without the turmoil of his physical presence. Dunny would never demand that she make up her mind. He would happily dangle after her forever. Really that was what she wanted. This had been the most wonderful period of her life, and she was in no rush to end it.

"Yes, you must go," she said with a sad look. "They say absence makes the heart grow fonder," she added enticingly.

"But of whom? I cannot like to leave you here alone with Dunsmore."

"I will not be alone, Griffin. Mama will be here to chaperon me."

Much good that would do him! He had a pretty clear idea which parti the mama favored. Alice, on the other hand, was in his camp. He would set her the job of watching out for his interests, and notifying him if that demmed sheep in sheep's clothing seemed to be gaining ground.

The sound of approaching footsteps warned them

that Mrs. Newbold was returning, and they drew apart.

Myra said, "Griffin has just been telling me that he must go to Mersham, Mama."

Good riddance! "Ah, and when must you leave?" the mama asked, damping down a hoot of joy.

"Tomorrow."

"Will you be gone long?"

"As the Season is nearly over, I expect you ladies will also be returning to Mersham soon. I had not planned to return to town in the immediate future. Perhaps a dashing visit from time to time, to tend to business." He went on to mention projected meetings with scientists and publishers.

Mrs. Newbold did some rapid conjecturing. The Season had a week to run. They would remain another week after to finish up the wedding plans, and Myra need not see Griffin again until she was a duchess. She would soon forget him if he was out of her sight.

"It is a pity you must run off so soon, Griffin. We shall notify you as soon as we return to Newbold Hall," the dame said, with every appearance of civility.

"I look forward to it. I trust you have no objection to my writing to Myra?"

Mrs. Newbold disliked it very much, but could not like to forbid it outright, or he might stay in town. "I see nothing amiss in that."

"I shall call before leaving tomorrow, in case you have any messages to be sent home," he said.

"Perhaps you would like to take breakfast with us?" Mrs. Newbold suggested. She felt a little like Pontius Pilate, for she had always liked Griffin, and he had taken her to meet the prince. Dunsmore, for all his connections, had never heeded that hint. But what she craved more than

59

anything else at that time was a dukedom for her daughter.

"Thank you, but I have adopted the habit of rising early, ma'am. In the wilds, there is no artificial light, you know. One lives close to nature, with the sun as the guide. I have a few meetings arranged for later in the morning. Will you be home around eleven?"

"We shall make it a point to be here." She thanked him for the wonderful evening and said good night.

Griffin hoped she would leave him a moment alone with Myra, but she stuck like a barnacle. He made his bows and left, unhappy with the outcome. He had promised himself he would get a straight answer before leaving. How had he let Myra wind him round her finger? It was her tears, of course . . . He never could be savage with a bawling woman.

"What took you so long?" Myra asked her mama, when they were alone.

"Sal has a sick stomach. Too much champagne, I wager."

"I thought you would never get back. Griffin demanded I make up my mind."

"What did you tell him?" the mama demanded in alarm.

"Oh, Mama, I could not decide. Perhaps when he is gone, I will be able to see things more clearly. He wanted to give me a diamond ring—a huge thing. It looked like a block of ice."

"You never liked big jewelry."

"No, it does not suit me. Rings, especially. I have small hands."

"A lady is wise to stick to what suits her. Great flashy things cause a stir, but there is something to be said for comfort over the long haul."

Her beady look told Myra that Mama was being clever. "Yes, Griffin is very handsome, but I never am comfortable when I am with him, somehow."

"Was Dunsmore planning to call tomorrow morning?"

Myra's fingers flew to her lips. "I forgot! He is coming for me at eleven. We were to drive to Bond Street."

"Put him off till afternoon. He will not complain when he learns the reason. Griffin was to accompany us to a few parties this next week. I wonder if it will be convenient for Dunsmore to take his place. Perhaps he has made other plans."

"Don't be silly, Mama. Of course he will accompany us."

"You must not take the duke for granted, dear. There is no saying he is not looking about for another girl, since he fears losing you. I noticed Lady Sara looking pretty sharp when you were laughing at Dunsmore tonight at the hotel. It would be just like her to go running to the duke with the story. She would not sit so long on her thumbs if she could wring an offer out of him."

This sly speech had exactly the desired effect. Myra was thrown into a fright, and dashed upstairs to write her note to Dunsmore at once, although she would not send it to him till morning.

Lord Griffin rushed through his business the next morning and called at ten-thirty. Alice had been informed of his leaving, and urged her mama to return to Newbold Hall.

"Peagoose! This is our chance to get Myra to choose Dunsmore."

"Don't you like Griffin, Mama? You were chirping merry when he proposed to Myra before he left for Brazil."

"I like him excessively, but I like Dunsmore better. It will not do you any harm, being chaperoned by a duchess next year, puss. There is no saying you won't nab a duke yourself. Or Dunsmore's cousin, the Marquess of Lansdowne."

Mrs. Newbold bustled off to speak to Cook. Myra remained abovestairs, putting the final touches to her toilette. Alice was alone in the saloon when Griffin arrived. For different reasons, they were both happy for a private visit.

Griffin hastened to the sofa and sat down, taking her two hands in his. "I want you to do a favor for me, Alice," he said, peering to the door. "I must go home, but I want you to keep an eye on Dunsmore and Myra. Try to keep them apart if you can."

She wrenched her hands away angrily. "I cannot do that! What excuse could I give?"

"You're right. That would not fadge. Naturally, he will attach himself to her apron strings the instant I am gone. If you could, perhaps, accompany them on their outings, or keep interrupting them when they are alone here, or—I don't know." He tossed up his hands in frustration. "Just look out for my interests. And most particularly, write to me at once if you sense Myra is leaning in his direction."

"It would be better if you could stay. Must you leave?"

"I should have gone home a week ago."

"It is too much responsibility," Alice objected. "I cannot *make* her fall in love with you, Griffin."

"She *is* in love with me," he said firmly. "I had her almost to the sticking point last night."

Alice damped down her alarm. "What about the ring?" She had already heard Myra's version, and was curious to hear it from Griffin's view.

"She did not refuse it. She liked it excessively."

"But she did not accept it."

"She needs a little more time."

"You said you were going to insist."

"Damme, she was crying. Do you take me for a brute?"

Her jeering smile caused a flush to darken his cheeks. "No, I begin to take you for as big a gudgeon as Dunsmore. Your long suit is manly bravado—derring-do, recklessness. If you are turning into a lapdog, you had best ask your good friend the Prince Regent to make you a duke, or you are outweighed."

"Next you will be granting that wilted weed the palm for looks as well."

"Not all ladies favor the blackamoor look," she said airily.

"That ain't the way it seems to me," he replied, his cockiness returning.

"How horrid—boasting! You were never conceited before, Griffin. I begin to think your notoriety has gone to your head. You are as bad as M—" She stopped herself in time, and strangely, Griffin did not appear to notice.

"What am I to think, when the ladies flock around me as if I were some rara avis?" he said.

"It seems odd that such a rare bird cannot win his lady," she taunted.

"I can only conclude your sister has some hankering to be a duchess. Dukes don't exactly grow on trees either. Will you help me, Alice?"

Alice resented being given this job, and said, "What makes you think I prefer you to Dunny for a brother-in-law?"

"Because you always had more sense than the other ladies in your family. I see you lifting your eyebrow at that compliment."

"I am trying to think of one single fact to support it."

"Well, you are a better rider, and you don't take forever to get dressed. You don't fly into the boughs if the coiffeur cuts your hair the wrong way, or become a watering pot if you see a bird with a broken wing."

"So I am badly turned out, and have no feelings!"

"Upon my word, you *have* grown up. You twist everything I say into an insult. Don't be difficult, Sal. I need your help, and so does Myra, or she will make the mistake of her life. Who do you think can make her happier? I, who love her madly, or Dunsmore?"

"Who worships the ground she walks on. You ask too much to expect me to keep them apart, when you cannot do it yourself, Griffin. They will have Mama's wholehearted support. She is sure to find some job for me if I take to pushing myself into their carriage. And at balls, you know, they will naturally stand up together. Besides, I have my own life. I have arranged several outings with my friends. I do not live in Myra's pocket."

"You're right," he admitted, abashed. "It was selfish of me to ask. It is hopeless."

He looked so dejected that she wanted to console him. "I shall keep a sharp eye on them, and write you at once if I fear she is succumbing to the ducal weed."

"God bless you." He leaned over, aiming a fleeting kiss at her cheek. It missed its mark and landed on her ear. A wave of heat invaded her head, then filtered slowly through her body. "I do love her so very much," he said, and drew a deep sigh.

"Why, Griffin?" she asked.

He just shook his head. "I don't know. It just happened, one day in the meadow at home. She was gathering bluebells on my land. I jokingly chided her. She looked so frightened, and so lovely.

64

It is not just her ethereal beauty I love, although she is ravishingly beautiful. Her hair like moonlight. I used to dream of her, while I slept by the fire in some Indian settlement, wishing she were by my side, to enjoy the splendor of the night sky, and the eerie jungle sounds in the background. One never knew what was prowling about—snakes, scorpions, wild boar."

"Myra would have hated it. She would have been thoroughly frightened."

"She would have had me to protect her." An image of the two of them, wrapped in a blanket against the night dangers, flashed into Alice's head to torment her.

Griffin continued, "Whenever I spotted a rare orchid growing in the forest, I would think of her, and ask myself what I was doing there. This is all my own fault. I stayed away too long. She has waited five years. It is selfish of me to insist she make up her mind in a week."

Myra and her mama joined them. Softened by his reminiscences, Griffin was gentle with Myra. She liked him in this tender mood, and was cast into doubts again.

Then Dunsmore arrived soon after Griffin left, and Myra also loved him. He had to be consoled for the stunt Griffin played on him the night before. That was the insensitive side of Griffin that she did not like. Dunny would never do such an underhanded thing. He was so very sweet and thoughtful. She smiled fondly on Dunny's engagement ring, that sat on her finger. It felt as comfortable as if it had grown there, unlike the great whopping diamond Griffin wanted her to wear. There was indeed something to be said for comfort.

Chapter Seven

Alice felt she had been hard on Griffin. If he truly loved Myra, the only thing she could do for him was to help him win her, and she made her best effort. She had plans to go out with Miss Sutton that morning and went to Bond Street, knowing Myra and Dunsmore always went there. Myra liked to dawdle along, looking at the shop windows. Miss Sutton, a saucy redhead, was deep in the throes of a passion for Griffin, so that Alice could at least talk about him.

When they met Myra and Dunsmore, Alice took Dunsmore's other arm and chatted to him, to prevent him from gaining ground with her sister. His conversation was yawningly dull. He pointed out bonnets and gewgaws in shop windows, and whatever their merits, invariably found them 'dashed pretty.' Strangely, it was Myra who first tired of the walk, and suggested they go home.

Dunsmore accompanied them to a rout party that evening. Myra developed a headache at midnight, and again went home early. A few days dragged on in this fashion. Myra, despite the unflagging devotion of her duke, was definitely in the mopes. Alice had no danger to report to Griffin, and thus had no excuse to write to him. Myra had received one letter, which she read in the privacy of her room, and carried in her pocket faithfully everywhere she went. She was occasionally spotted mooning over it in some quiet corner.

On the forth evening of Griffin's absence, Alice went to her sister's room for a coze after an outing. Once more, Myra was studying the letter.

"Reading Griffin's letter again. You must have it by heart," Alice said. She was extremely curious to see it, but knew this was unlikely.

"It is a marvelous letter," Myra sighed. "So passionate, so poetic. Griffin could be a poet, if he took the bother."

"Are you missing him very much?"

"Terribly. I feel a dull and aching void where my heart should be." She clutched at her breast and drew a shuddering sigh.

"Good Lord, Myra. It is unlike you to speak of dull and aching voids."

"It is what Griffin says, and I feel exactly the same. Everything seems so dull without him." Alice's heart sank to her toes. "People do not flock around me and Dunsmore the way they did when I went out with Griffin. You must have noticed, Alice, at the balls. Do you not remember that current of excitement when I stood up with him, or even with Dunsmore? Every eye was on me. All that is lacking now that Griffin is gone."

"It sounds as if you are missing the adulation, not Griffin."

"It is one and the same thing, really. He makes me special in a way that Dunny, much as I love him, does not."

"Then why do you not accept Griffin and put him out of his misery?"

A flash of anger darted in Myra's eyes. "And hand the duke over to Lady Sara? Did you see the way she was chasing him at the rout tonight? I never saw anyone so brass-faced in my life. She asked him to stand up with her. Your friend Miss Sutton would not hesitate to nab him either, if she had the chance. I daresay it was her idea that you and she join us on the strut earlier this week. She has the nerve of a canal horse."

Alice swallowed her mirth at the absurdity of Sukey Sutton liking Dunsmore. "You cannot have them both, Myra," she said simply. "And you cannot dangle them on the string much longer."

"Oh, you are just like him," Myra scolded, fingering the letter from Griffin. "He is nagging me to make up my mind, too. It is *impossible*. I thought when he went to Mersham, I would fall fatally in love with Dunsmore, but it was just the opposite. I think I am falling out of love with him, Alice. What shall I do? I know Mama favors Dunny."

"It is not Mama who will have to live with him."

"*Have* to live with him? You make it sound like a penance. Dunsmore Castle is one of the finest estates in Britain, to say nothing of his hunting box, and his Hampshire estate and his London residence, much finer than Griffin's. *Have* to live with him, indeed!"

"You said you were falling out of love with him."

"That is not what I meant," Myra said vaguely. "Of course I love him. I love Griffin, too, but in a different way. He is so—" She came to a discreet stop.

"What?" Alice demanded.

"He kisses like a tiger, Alice," she said, and gave

a frightened shudder of delight. "It stirred me to the core. I nearly died of excitement."

"You should not let him kiss you in that way. Not till you are married."

"I am engaged to him."

"You are engaged to Dunsmore, too. If Mama knew about this she would—"

"Don't you dare tell her. Anyway, what has it to do with you? I begin to suspect you are in love with him yourself." Alice flushed bright pink. "I knew it! I saw how you grabbed on to his arm on Bond Street, and dragged him off to look at all the windows. My own sister! How could you?"

Alice realized the mistake, and laughed in giddy relief. "Don't be ridiculous. Dunsmore is not my type at all."

"You can be sure you are not his. He thinks you are a hoyden."

"And I think he is a dead bore," Alice said saucily, and bounced out of the room.

She went to bed and lay awake long, thinking. If being away from Griffin had made Myra fonder of him, then perhaps being away from Dunsmore might make Myra fall in love with her duke. Throw in a soupçon of jealousy from Lady Sara, and who knew what might result? On the other hand, if they returned to Newbold, Griffin's tigerish embrace might finally nudge Myra into having him. Either way, it had to be settled, but in her deepest heart, Alice truly did not think Myra would make Griffin happy for long. They did not suit; they were totally opposite in disposition.

She finally slept, and had disturbing dreams of tigers who refused to maul her, though she lay wounded and helpless in the jungle, staring at the wild black sky, sprinkled with diamonds. She went downstairs in the morning, still tired and on the fidgets. Her mother examined her and said, "I begin to think Myra is right."

Alice looked up guiltily, wondering if Myra had figured out her secret. "What do you mean, Mama?"

"You look worn to the bone. So does Myra. She says she is tired of London, and wants to go home to Newbold Hall."

"What about Dunsmore?" Alice asked.

"Naturally he will come with us. I am not fool enough to deliver her, helpless, into Griffin's clutches."

Alice considered this a moment, and thought the plan was rife with potential trouble. "She just wants to lord it in the village with her two fiancés," she said dismissingly. "Let us go home if she wants, but it would look very odd to drag Dunsmore along."

"What is odd about a fiancé visiting the family of his bride to be, miss?"

"You know what I mean."

"I shall sound Dunsmore out when he calls this morning. If he thinks it farouche, then we shall stay on in London. Dunsmore would never agree to anything in poor taste."

"This is a horrid idea, Mama, and you know it. It will end up in a duel. It is just Myra's craving for attention. Separate her from the duke for a spell, and you will achieve better results."

"Aye, but who is to keep Griffin from her skirt tails if she goes home alone? I don't trust that lad an inch. There is mischief lurking in him. You have only to look at his black eyes to see it."

"She will not be alone. You and I will be there."

"Griffin would pay as much attention to us as he pays to that white monkey. If your papa were alive . . ."

"Do you really think Dunsmore could handle him?"

"No more than a flea could handle a dog. Lord, I have the megrims already, and it is not yet nine o'clock. I wish Griffin had stayed in the jungle with the rest of the wild animals."

Dunsmore called at eleven. When Myra presented the plan of going to Newbold Hall, he agreed instantly. Her manner of delivering the invitation may have had something to do with his acceptance.

"Mama is taking me home to Newbold Hall, Dunny. I do hope you will come with us, or Griffin may . . ." She gave a helpless sigh. "You know what I mean. But if *you* were there—"

"Aye, the shoe would be on the other side of the foot," he said. His courage had a way of soaring when Griffin was not within shooting distance. Dunny was fully aware of the tigerish attack of his rival. Myra kept no secrets from him. "I shan't leave your side for an instant," he promised.

The postman brought Myra another billet-doux from Griffin, and she ran upstairs to read it in her room. She was disappointed to see the first page was full of the word Monty, and dull estate matters. The second page, however, was more satisfying. It brought a tingle of that remembered excitement.

Dunsmore was so worried when Myra returned with shining eyes and pink cheeks, clutching the billet-doux to her bosom, that he would have agreed to go to Brazil, if that was what she wanted. It was arranged that they would leave early the next morning, to arrive in mid-afternoon at Newbold Hall. The remainder of the day was occupied with canceling appointments and settling household matters.

Mrs. Newbold hoped that when she returned to

town, it would be to arrange the final details of Myra's marriage to Dunsmore. The invitations sat in a pile, awaiting delivery or consignment to the grate, depending on Myra's decision. They should have been delivered by now, but society would be lenient. Everyone was aware of her enviable dilemma. The reservation of St. George's church for the wedding had not been canceled. The plans for dinner at the Pulteny remained in place. One way or the other, there would be a wedding, but if Griffin was chosen, the invitations would have to be redone. One could hardly scratch out the groom's name and write in the replacement by hand. And, of course, many of the guests would be changed. She would lose such worthies as the Marquess of Lansdowne, though Griffin's family were by no means contemptible.

The trip was arranged so hastily that Alice hadn't time to notify Griffin. They would be home as fast as the letter could reach him. She would get a message to him the minute they arrived at Newbold.

Myra drove in Dunsmore's carriage with her mama. Both ladies were conscious of the strawberry leaves decorating the door. Alice chose to drive with her mama's dresser in their family carriage. She hoped for peace and quiet to torture herself with thoughts of Myra and Griffin. She was given no quiet, but considerable assistance in her woeful repining. Mrs. Appleton chattered the whole way about schemes to bring Griffin to the fore. As a longtime resident at Newbold, she had a high opinion of Lord Griffin.

"Lord Griffin will not be outdone," she forecast cheerfully. "Don't mope, child. Once your sister sees the two of them together in the country, she will make the proper decision. What is there to choose between that long drink of water and Griffin? Your mama was mad to bring the duke to the country, where he will be forced onto horseback, and terrified by dogs. Griffin on horseback—who could say him nay?"

"I had not thought of that!" Alice said in alarm.

"Nor had your mama, I warrant," Mrs. Appleton said, and laughed merrily.

Chapter Eight

During the commotion of arrival, Alice asked a servant to have her mount saddled up. No one thought it strange that this farouche creature should choose to ride in lieu of taking tea, on a fine spring day. She had complained constantly in London that she missed her riding. In fact, she rode two days out of three, but to Alice, a sedate trot along Rotten Row bore about as much resemblance to riding as a twig to a tree.

She did not wait to have her riding habit unpacked, but wore the old one she had left hanging in her clothespress at home. It was a faded blue, out of date, well-worn, and a trifle snug. She would have preferred wearing her new one to impress Griffin, but it was at the bottom of her trunk. Within a quarter of an hour of arriving, she was cantering across the meadow to Mersham on her bay mare.

It was a fine day. The sun shone in a cerulean sky, scudded with white puffs of cloud. A warming zephyr caressed her cheeks, and lifted her skirt.

When she passed into Griffin's meadow, she remembered where the bluebells grew, and thought of Griffin's falling in love with Myra there. It was odd Myra should have been there alone, as she usually took her walks in their own park. If only Myra had stayed home that day, everything might have been different. It was odd how one little thing should change so many lives. When she roused herself from this reverie, Mersham shimmered before her like a fairy castle.

Little survived of the original thirteenth-century Cistercian abbey. Over the centuries, it had been subjected to cannonball, fire, and depredation. In fact, the dower house standing a thousand feet from it was said to have been built of the stones from the west wing of the original abbey. But the main building looked very old to Alice, and was imbued with romance. She thought it the most beautiful house in all of England.

Sprawling wings of weathered stone stood out against the blue sky and greenery of the park. There were lancet windows in front, but her approach from the west gave her a view of long casement windows, with the famous Mersham terraced gardens below, leading to an *allée* of poplars and terminating in a man-made lake. Griffin had taught her how to catch tadpoles there when she was young. She still looked for them every spring, but no longer took them home in a bottle.

She hoped she would find Griffin outdoors on this fine day. If she went to the house, she would have to deal with Monty, or perhaps Lady Griffin was back at home by now. Alice circled the terraced gardens on her way to the stable. The flowers were in full bloom. She stopped to admire a purple cloud of campanulas, backed by a profusion of roses. A drift of some white blooms seemed to rest on top of a stone wall. She knew they actually grew on the other side of the wall.

In the distance, flowers of all hues spread like a painting before her, with patches of white flowers and greenery acting as a buffer to the colored areas. The air was heavy with perfume. She continued reluctantly around to the stable. Lafferty, the groom, recognized her at once. "Is Griffin at home?" she asked.

"His lordship's gone to a horse auction, miss. Should be home any time now."

"He did not waste much time," Alice said, smiling in approval.

"There's been nothing fit for a gentleman to throw a leg over since Mr. Montgomery took over. Things'll change now."

They gossiped for five minutes. Alice heard that Montgomery was still at Mersham. The expected blowup had not occurred, except for a bit of a holler over her ladyship's being in the dower house. While they were chatting, Griffin arrived, riding a showy bay gelding.

"Alice, what are you doing here? Is Myra home?" he asked. A hopeful smile beamed.

"Yes, we just arrived. I would like a word with you, Griffin, if you are free."

Alice had to admire the gelding's points before opening her budget. It was a fine animal, fiery of eye, long and trim of limb, and deep-chested.

"Would you like to go in and say hello to Mama?" Griffin said.

"Not just now, Griffin. I have something to tell you."

His eyes flew open in alarm. He took her by the elbow to hasten her away from the groom's ears. They strolled toward the lake. "She hasn't accepted him!" Griffin asked. She read the horror in his eyes.

"No."

The tension eased out of his body, and a small smile of triumph lifted his lips. "You frightened the wits out of me, brat. If she has come home early, then surely—"

"She brought Dunsmore with her."

"What!" It was an angry howl of dismay.

"She brought him to Newbold."

"Then she must have accepted him."

"No, no."

"Why else would he be here?"

"She's still trying to make up her mind," Alice said, ashamed to say it.

Griffin uttered a few oaths and kicked a stone so hard he broke the leather on the toe of his top boot. "She takes the lady's prerogative of indecision too far."

"It is a pity she left London, for she was quite falling in love with you when you were away."

"Really?" His first smile soon faded to a frown. "I fear that is a somewhat ambiguous compliment. Can she not love me when I am *near*? Must I return to Brazil to win her?"

"At least it would enable you to travel some more," she said, trying to lighten the air.

"I am through with buzzing around the world," he said, but he said it wistfully.

They reached the lake, and sat on a large table rock by its edge. Griffin gazed into the still water, frowning. "I should have forced her to a decision before I left, as I intended to."

"Take heart, Griffin. Dunsmore will be like a fish out of water in the countryside. He is a wretched rider. He looks like a stick on horseback. You are at your best in the country. Make a dashing toilette and go cantering up to her, mounted on your new gelding. He is a fine animal, by the by. Has he a name?"

"He is called Lightening," he replied distractedly.

"I expect you will be looking for a hunter as well?"

"Yes. What is she doing now, Alice?"

"Probably having tea. We just arrived. I came straight over to tell you."

"What an excellent helper you are! You must be wanting your tea, too. Why won't you come in and say hello to Mama? She would like to see you."

"Another time. Tomorrow perhaps," she replied.

He nodded, still distracted. "She did not even send me a note, to let me know she is home," he said.

"She will. Give her time to settle in. Why do you not come over this evening?"

Griffin's jaw firmed in decision. "I shan't call until she lets me know she is here, and asks me to come."

"Then I shall look forward to seeing you this evening. And now I shall really go for a ride. That was my excuse to get away."

"Am I turning you into a deceiver, with my machinations?"

"Good gracious, no! I have always been a deceiver," she replied airily.

"Not you, Sal. Unlike most ladies, you say what you mean, and mean what you say. Even when you picked Mama's rare Queen Charlotte roses, that she was nurturing for a prize, you owned up to it."

"Unfortunately, integrity does not seem to count for much with gentlemen," she retorted sharply.

He looked surprised. "Were you not boasting of your conquests in London? I am surprised you escaped without being caught."

"I had two offers," she said, "but it was not my integrity the gentlemen liked. In one case it was my dowry, and in the other, it was my amiability. Mr. Jenkins told me I was the most amiable girl he ever met."

"There is something to be said for an amiable girl," Griffin said. He smiled ruefully and seized her hand. Alice, in her outmoded habit, still looked like a child to him. "Anyway, there is no rush, Sal. You are young."

She withdrew her hand. He noticed a flush invade her cheeks. Why did a reminder of their precious youth invariably annoy young ladies? He also noticed that a very feminine body was pressing against the material of her too small riding habit. He found it strangely exciting.

"I was eighteen last month, Griffin. My mama was married when she was seventeen."

"Good Lord, eighteen! And I can give you a decade. Sometimes it seems I left England a young sprout, and returned an old man. It is high time I marry and set up a nursery. Monty's taking over Mersham has reminded me of my mortality. I should like my son to assume the estate when I die."

"The groom said Monty is still at Mersham."

"Yes, until he makes other arrangements. You were right about his being a good guardian, Sal."

"He is highly spoken of hereabouts. We were worried when he took charge, but really it was a benefit in disguise. Your mama takes an interest in the gardens, but seemed all adrift about other estate matters."

"He devoted every minute to his duties. One cannot accuse him of slacking. We Griffins always spent too much time on horticulture. Monty has squeezed the purse strings tightly. A little more tightly than I like, actually, but the extra savings will enable me to right a few wrongs."

"What do you mean?"

"He retired three elderly servants on a very miserly pension. Sold off my spare cattle. There was nothing in the stable but one carriage team and his own hack. I notice he is also scrimping on gardeners. Mama used to hire a dozen local fellows to give the gardeners a hand in the busy season. The gardens have always been a feature of Mersham. All that can be remedied, however. Monty was a wise investor."

"The gardens still look very nice. I noticed them as I drove up."

"Oh yes, he kept the chief gardener on, and allowed him a few assistants. It still looks well enough, but a garden such as ours is not only maintained, it is constantly being improved. I look forward to getting my South American specimens going. I daresay I shall have to enlarge the conservatory."

Alice listened attentively. "It will be hard for Monty, losing out on Mersham."

"I shan't leave him penniless, but my heart hardens when I consider his haste in removing Mama to the dower house. He didn't even fix it up for her."

"Who is at the dower house now?"

"It is empty. Monty suggested I lease it. I am not sure I want a stranger so close to Mersham."

"Why don't you let Monty stay there?" she suggested.

"I doubt he would want to. He'll be looking for a job. I shan't hesitate to give him a good character."

"Why don't you hire him to look after Mersham, under your supervision so that he does not become too thrifty? You said he is an able manager, and you will want to devote plenty of time to the conservatory. He is acquainted with the place now, and has made friends locally. I wager he would jump at the offer."

Griffin looked interested. "That is not a bad idea, Sal. I shall put it to him. And if I can talk Myra into a honeymoon in Italy, it will be well to have Monty looking after things here."

"She didn't mention a honeymoon in Italy! How lovely!"

"I have not dared to mention it to her. She dislikes the notion of my darting off alone—I can understand that, but that is not to say we could not go on a civilized sort of journey together. And Greece is so close, I hope to talk her into a side trip there. I should like to roam the rock cliffs of Greece, gathering specimens of wildflowers."

"I should like to see the ruins. To sit in one of those old amphitheaters and listen to someone declaiming below. Mr. Jenkins said you can hear a pin drop." She stopped and narrowed her eyes at him. "But roaming cliffs? This honeymoon is beginning to sound less civilized, and less likely to attract Myra," she warned.

"If Greece is not civilized, I should like to know what is. It is the very cradle of Western civilization."

"That is mere sophistry, sir. You know very well ruins and roaming cliffs are not Myra's idea of civilization. Balls and plays and concerts now—does Greece have such amenities?"

"You've got me there, Sal, but Italy certainly has. If I agree to the balls and plays and concerts, she must give way to something, too. Marriage involves compromises."

Alice rose. "That is for you two lovebirds to argue out between you. I am merely the messenger. And we know what happens to messengers," she added.

Griffin also stood up and began accompanying her back to the stable. "Only when they bring bad news. I do feel, however, that news of Myra's arrival ought to have come from herself. Perhaps there is a note waiting for me."

Alice did not encourage him in this hope. She felt quite certain Myra would not have written yet. "I look forward to seeing you soon at Newbold."

He lifted her onto her mount, as he had often done in the past. As his hands closed around her waist, he was conscious of the soft flare of hips, and the gentle swell of her bosoms. He was also aware of a strange stirring within him.

"You are getting a little large for me to lift you," he said, embarrassed lest his thoughts were evident.

"Next time I shall use the mounting block." He noticed the conscious look in her eyes, and knew she felt this new awareness, too.

The groom, watching, chewed back a smile. "It was your leaving that did the harm, milord. Folks do say that if a fellow lifts a heifer when she is newborn and keeps doing so every day, he can eventually lift a full-grown cow."

"Thank you for calling me a cow, Lafferty!" Alice said, and urged her mount forward.

"She's all growed up," Lafferty said, and returned to his duties.

Griffin looked after Alice as she dashed toward the park. She was totally at home on horseback. He watched as her straight back and proud little head disappeared around a corner. A pity Myra was not a little more like her. He remembered that Myra did not ride if she could help it. She did not go in much for any physical activity except dancing. If it were Sal he was in love with, there would be no arguing necessary about the trip to Greece. He had an inkling Sal would love it.

Chapter Nine

"Have you let Griffin know you are home?" Alice asked, as the sisters went belowstairs to dinner that evening. She had not told anyone of her trip to Mersham, and with a duke to be entertained, it did not occur to anyone to ask her.

"I shall let him know tomorrow. Dunny and I wanted one evening alone first," Myra replied blandly.

"It is only common courtesy to tell him, before he hears it in the village. I think you should write to him now."

"It is time for dinner."

"It wouldn't take a minute."

"No, no. He will come the minute I write. I am too tired to face him tonight. There is no hurry. I shall write tomorrow morning."

Alice felt a sting of anger at that complacent, *He will come the minute I write.* Yet it was true. "What of the aching void in your heart?" she asked snidely.

"Mama said he should not have written such warm things."

"You showed his letters to Mama!" Alice exclaimed.

"Of course I did."

As they were not considered private, Alice was eager to read Griffin's outpourings herself. "Can I see them?"

"Certainly not. You are too young."

"You may be older, but you are no wiser, Myra. You should have let Griffin know you are home. Don't wait any longer than tomorrow, or he will be in a wretched temper," she said curtly.

Myra smiled her gloating smile. "I shouldn't think so, Alice. He will be happy to see me, as he expected me to stay in London for another week at least. Anyway, what concern is it of yours?" She did not wait for a reply, but flounced into the saloon.

There were no guests for dinner the first evening. Dinner was quiet to the point of tedium. The duke was nervous about Griffin; Mrs. Newbold was nervous at having the duke as a guest; Alice was irritated, and Myra was distracted. What little conversation there was centered around Griffin.

"Daresay he will wonder why I am here," the duke said, stirring his potatoes into a mound, but not eating them.

"He will know why you are here, Duke," Alice said.

"That is true, but we shan't make an issue of it. I mean to say—when you see him, Myra, you might just—" Alice smiled into her collar. The duke saw her sly smile, and blushed. "Whatever you say, be sure you say nothing. To upset him, I mean. We do not want any scandal. Mama hates anything in the way of a brouhaha." He frowned in consternation. That did not sound quite right, somehow.

"Try the capon, Your Grace," Mrs. Newbold said. "You will like it." Now what was that *chit* of an Alice smirking about?

After dinner, the ladies and the duke gathered in the saloon for a game of whist, only to learn that His Grace scarcely knew a spade from a club. With nothing better to do, they played cards anyway.

"Heh heh, nothing to it," the duke said, gathering up Mrs. Newbold's trick. "It is as easy as chopping off a log."

She was too nice to point out his error. A commanding glare at her younger daughter kept Alice from telling him, and the game continued in this haphazard fashion.

Alice was on pins, wondering if Griffin would come. Good to his word, he stayed at home, pacing the saloon like a caged lion, and giving his mama a case of the fidgets.

"Either go to see her or sit down, James," Lady Griffin said, after enduring twenty minutes of his frenzied pacing. "You are wearing out the carpet."

Lady Griffin was happy to be back in her own saloon. She was tall, dark, and handsome, like her son. Gravity was beginning to get the better of this faded beauty's chin and jaws, but her eyes were still brightly alert. She especially enjoyed having Monty to lord it over, after his shabby treatment of her. At the moment, she was pretending to read the *Morning Observer*, for no reason but to keep it from him.

Montgomery, although he was only in his late thirties, wore the wizened appearance of the nip farthing. He shared some physical resemblance to the Griffins—mostly height and coloring—but his features were sharper.

"Would you like to go over the current accounts, Griffin?" he asked.

"Not tonight, Monty." Griffin continued pacing back and forth in front of the fireplaces at either end of the gold saloon, never glancing at the splendor around him. Molded ceilings, fine furnishings wearing the patina of age and beeswax, an Oriental carpet and a set of matching Van Dykes of his ancestors went unnoticed.

Why did she not write? She was with Dunsmore, holed up in some corner, whispering sweet nothings, while her mama smiled in approval. Had Myra only come home to torment him? On his next trip toward the door, he kept walking.

"Going to Newbold, are you?" Lady Griffin called.

"I shall be in the conservatory, if any message comes for me," he called back, and kept walking.

"A hand of cards, Mr. Montgomery?" Lady Griffin asked. She knew Monty hated cards. She also knew he hoped to be given the dower house, and was thus on his best behavior. Griffin had not told him the news yet. Lady Griffin thought it an excellent plan, although she had no intention of letting Monty run tame at Mersham once he had his own house.

"Delightful," Monty said dutifully, and went to get the game table.

In his conservatory, Griffin sorted through the specimens he had collected in Brazil and carefully nurtured until he got them home. Some of them were small rooted plants carefully dug out of the earth and transplanted into pots; others were cuttings he had kept in moist cotton to root, but most were seeds. Each seed bag bore a tag of identification, along with his sketch of the mature plant and its preferred soil and light requirement. He was doing research to see if some of them might endure outdoor planting in England's cooler climate. That brick wall that caught the afternoon sun would hold the warmth for hours, and protect fragile plants from wind. He would try some of his exotic specimens there.

The bananas, of which he had become fond while in Brazil, he feared would not weather outdoors. He had brought home six different types. Brontley, the president of the horticultural club, had told him bananas were herbs, although they looked for the world like trees. Nature was full of surprises.

His worries about Myra and the duke faded as he immersed himself in the world of plants. He felt at home here, with the smell of the earth and the whispering leaves all around him. His head gardener, MacIver, had weaseled a box of geraniums of some new species out of his friend at Kew. A dozen of them had been used for cuttings. The small plants, forty-eight in all, sat on the end of a table, awaiting planting. The flowers were just beginning to open. Slivers of red showed through the closed heads. The perfume of gardenias in full bloom hung heavy on the air. When he glanced at his watch, it was ten-thirty, and too late to hope to hear from Myra that night. Why had she not sent for him?

His neck was cramped and his feet full of pins and needles from sitting on an uncomfortable stool. He walked down the rows of palms, imagining he was back in the jungle. But try as he might, he could not imagine Myra with him. His heart wrenched at the memory of those long, lonesome nights without her, longing for her. That was just dreaming; Myra would never go to such a place. Sal, perhaps . . . She would not be afraid of the odd snake or Indian. A smile curved his lips. Perhaps if Sal accompanied them on their honeymoon, Myra would not balk at Greece. He must be mad, to think of bringing that imp on his honeymoon.

But he would have a honeymoon, and soon. If not

Myra, then he must choose another lady. London was full of lovely and venturesome ladies. There was Lady Sara Winsley, and that pretty redheaded girl Alice ran around with. Miss Sutton, was it? Both of them had been rolling their sparkling eyes at him. Yes, by God, he would do it. He would give Myra an ultimatum the next time they met. The duke or himself; he would wait no longer. But he did hope she would choose him.

The next morning, Myra went for her bonnet and pelisse after breakfast. "Dunny and I are driving into the village, Mama. Is there anything you need?" she asked.

"Have you written to Griffin?" Alice asked.

"I shall, as soon as I return."

"You should let him know, Myra."

"He will be busy in the morning. She can write when she comes back," Mrs. Newbold said, and began scratching up a list of a few items she required.

Alice wanted to renew acquaintances in the village, and asked if she might go with them. In fact, she admitted to herself that she wanted to be seen in Headcorn in the carriage with the prestigious strawberry leaves on the door, too.

"Certainly, why not?" Myra said pleasantly.

The duke expressed his pleasure with the idea as well, and in minutes the three of them were darting along in the well-sprung chaise, receiving all the attention they could wish. When they got down from the carriage, they could scarcely walk a step without being accosted by curious villagers. These friends were all too awestruck by the ladies' new London fashions and by the duke to inquire about Myra's other fiancé, but their curiosity was visible on their faces. Myra had not enjoyed herself so much since strutting on Bond Street with Griffin.

Here, she and her duke received the same fawning attention without Griffin.

Myra began to think that she could have the best of both worlds if she rejected Griffin, and he went brokenhearted back to the jungles of Brazil, renouncing civilization entirely. In her mind, the idea had mythic overtones. She saw herself as a sort of goddess of love, inciting hopeless passions in aching hearts around the world. Griffin would discover wonderful new flowers and name them for her. When word of his death reached England, people would send her condolences, as if she were his widow, and Dunny would comfort her. She would wear mourning gowns, or perhaps half mourning. She looked well in violet.

She dragged the duke into the drapery shop, where she could denigrate the goods with the practiced eye of a London shopper. She did manage to find a few bits of lace and ribbon to tempt her, and as the parcels were small, the duke could carry them as well as Mama's parcels.

Alice left them for a quick visit with Nancy Warwick, a bosom bow who had not enjoyed the glory of a Season. They both kept an eye on the window, and when Myra and the duke came out of the drapery shop, Alice jumped up. "I have to go now, Nancy. Come out and see me soon. I daresay we shall be having routs and things at Newbold, since we have to entertain the duke."

"Let me know which one Myra chooses," Nancy said. A strangled sound came out of her throat.

Alice peered to see what caused it. "Lord Griffin!" she said, in a weak voice.

He was advancing at a stiff gait toward Myra and the duke. Even from across the street, Alice could sense the anger roiling within him. "I must go," she said, and tore out of the house in an effort to divert disaster.

Griffin had spotted Myra and Dunsmore before they saw him, and immediately strode up to them. "Good morning, my dear," he said, lifting his hat. "Dunsmore," he added, a cool glance just flickering off the duke, before he returned his attention to Myra. "What a delightful and unexpected surprise. Have you been at Newbold long?"

Myra read the damped anger in his eyes, and trembled. "No! We just arrived, didn't we, Dunny?"

"Yes, by Jove."

"You must have left London in the middle of the night!" Griffin said.

"We arrived late yesterday, actually," Myra said. "I was about to write to you."

"When?" His eyes were an accusation.

"As soon as I got home."

"I see shopping takes precedence." He directed a speaking glance at the bundles in the duke's arms.

The duke, flustered, dropped a bag, and while retrieving it, dropped two others.

Griffin ignored him. "When will it be convenient for me to call, ma'am?" he asked, in a voice stiff with disapproval.

Myra felt at that moment that she never wanted him to call. She spotted Alice flying across the street and turned to her as to a rescuer. "Here is Alice," she said.

Griffin also ignored this. "When?" he repeated.

"You can come this evening," Myra said, and gave the teetering parcels in Dunsmore's arms a pat.

"Very kind of you," he said, his lips white with fury. *You can come,* as if he were a beggar. He would come all right!

"Come for dinner, Griffin," Alice said, leveling a commanding look on her sister.

"By all means, if you have not made other plans," Myra added.

Griffin's black eyes measured the duke. "No plans that preclude you—and the duke. I look forward to it."

Dunsmore was thrown into spasms of dread by that look. It was as frightening as a death knell. He must do something to ingratiate this savage. "We look forward to hearing about your Brazilian adventures, what? Perhaps you could show us some of your—er, some of the things you brought home."

"You should have attended my lectures in London, Dunsmore. I am not accustomed to sing for my supper when my fiancée invites me to dine." Griffin lifted his hat, glared balefully at the duke, and proceeded on his way.

"I say, did you have to ask him to dinner?" Dunsmore said, in a small voice. "He looked ready to take a bite out of me."

"Silly," Myra laughed. "What can he do?"

"I wonder if he brought his spear to Mersham," Alice said mischievously.

Myra and the duke exchanged a frightened look and hastened to the inn, and the safety of the strawberry leaves.

Chapter Ten

Mrs. Newbold was not so lacking in propriety that she failed to send a dinner invitation to Lady Griffin, when she learned that Griffin was to dine with them that evening.

"I suppose I must go," Lady Griffin said, upon reading the note.

"Suit yourself, Mama. The duke especially asked that I tell him about Brazil, and bring some of my treasures to entertain the folks. You have seen and heard all that."

"It is bound to be unpleasant, one way or the other," she said consideringly.

"Is that a slur on my powers of entertainment?" he teased.

"Certainly not, dear. I enjoyed your bizarre tales the first half dozen times. I do hope you are not going to grow into one of those prosy old bores, like retired generals, who are forever reliving their perilous adventures in public. No, what I meant, actually, is that you and the duke will slog it out about Myra. You must not issue a challenge, my dear. You know my niece is married to Dunsmore's uncle, or some such thing. We are connected anyhow, and it would be excessively bad *ton* to kill a duke, though I daresay society would give you a medal."

"I shan't challenge him, but I do intend to get the matter settled this evening, one way or the other."

"It is really the outside of enough that that prissy young lady is bearleading you and the duke. Oh, I grant you she is pretty, but she is the sort whose jaw will advance as she ages. I detect a trace of the Hapsburg jaw in that lady, James. Then her nose will descend, and those blue eyes fade quickly."

"Don't be foolish. She is the most beautiful lady in England."

"She is beautiful *now*, but hers is not the sort of beauty that lasts, like some." She waited for a compliment on the endurance of her own beauty. When it did not come, she continued, "Lady Calmet, for example, is still a handsome creature, and she is pushing sixty. You could always offer for her daughter, Lady Sara, if Myra turns you off. I am amazed someone has not snatched Sara up before now. They say she has every imaginable accomplishment."

"You are being a tad previous, Mama. Myra has not turned me off yet."

"Let me know her answer when you get home. Tell the Newbolds I have a headache. This is the last evening I shall have to pay back Monty, and I mean to put it to good use. By tomorrow night, he will be at the dower house. Ha, now he will regret not fixing it up for me! The place is like a dungeon. It needs redoing from top to bottom."

"I am sure Monty will do all that needs doing.

He is a frightful nipcheese, but only remember all the money he made for us."

"Yes, I daresay it is good business to hire him, but if you go abroad again, dear, write frequently, so that we do not take the notion the savages have made a fricassee of you, or Monty will move himself in as your heir again. What barbaric rubbish will you take to entertain the guests this evening?"

"Myself, primarily. As I consider the likely lack of conversation, however, perhaps I shall take along a few other farouche items as well."

"Don't take those horrid *macumba* things, dear. They kept me awake for hours. I find myself burning the hair from my brushes, in case my dresser gets hold of it and puts it on one of those dolls the natives from Bahia stick pins in."

"Those African religious cult stories usually bring the house down," he said unconcernedly.

"I am sure they do, dear, but a hostess has no particular desire to have her house brought down around her ears."

"You take me too literally, Mama."

"A gentleman says what he means, James."

"Pity a lady don't," he retorted, and wandered off to his room.

Griffin made a careful toilette before going to Newbold. He was not immodest, but he knew that physically, he was vastly superior to the duke. He would win Myra by his handsome face and his lively conversation. He would charm her by tales of the beauty of Brazil—and perhaps even induce in her a wish to travel . . .

Griffin regretted his uncivil treatment of Dunsmore, and took along a few of his Brazilian artifacts to make up for it. He had a small trunk of them still packed from his London lectures, and had the trunk put into the carriage. No time had been specified for arrival, but Newbold kept country hours, and he went at six o'clock. He was greeted by Mrs. Newbold and Alice.

"We have put dinner off till seven, since the duke is with us," Mrs. Newbold explained. "Myra took Dunsmore to call on the vicar. He is going to give Dunsmore a tour of the church tomorrow. The vicar will be coming back with them for dinner." She had augmented the dinner party to include a few neighbors, to show off the duke, and to divert the likelihood of disaster. Myra had given her a vivid account of the meeting in Headcorn.

"They should be home any minute," Alice added, when she saw Griffin's hackles rising. "What is that trunk your footman brought in?"

"Dunsmore asked me to bring some of my keepsakes, you recall." She also recalled Griffin's sharp retort, and smiled to show her appreciation of his compliance.

"Why do you not put it in the small parlor?" Mrs. Newbold suggested. She did not want her saloon littered with spears and shields when her guests arrived.

Griffin directed his footman to take the trunk there. Meanwhile some other guests arrived to wile away the hour till dinner was served. Myra and Dunsmore got home in time to change for dinner at seven. When they saw Griffin's carriage in the stable, they sneaked in by the kitchen door and up the servants's stairs to change. They both felt very wicked and daring. Griffin's pursuit of Myra had that advantage of enlivening what was otherwise a rather dull courting.

The seating arrangement for dinner had been a nuisance to the hostess. The duke, of course, took precedence over everyone else. She put him at her right hand and Myra's other fiancé at her left.

There was, alas, only one Myra, and she insisted on sitting beside the duke. To make it up to Griffin, she gave him her prettiest guest, Mrs. Arbuthnot, for a companion. This young widow was the local dasher, who would not normally get to put her feet under Mrs. Newbold's table. Desperate measures were called for, however, and Mrs. Arbuthnot was an extremely pretty redhead not much older than Griffin. Hopefully, she would keep him in curl.

This lively creature kept Griffin amused over dinner by the simple expedient of smiling in adoration, and making approving sounds at his every utterance. What she did not achieve was to prevent him from noticing and resenting the mama's seating arrangement. A slow anger was building in him. Flirting openly with Mrs. Arbuthnot did not begin to dissipate it. When he occasionally caught Alice's eye, glaring balefully at him across the table, he flirted all the harder.

With a promise of seeing Griffin's treasures after dinner, the gentlemen did not remain long at their port. By nine-thirty they had rejoined the ladies in the saloon, and all were ready to be entertained.

Griffin spoke first of his own interest, the flowers and trees of South America. As interest dwindled noticeably, he had the trunk brought into the saloon, and began displaying the various objects, speaking a little about each one. Some uncut diamonds roused the ladies to interest. They all agreed they looked like ordinary pebbles. He brought forth a geological formation that looked on the outside like a big, rough coconut. It was called a geode, and had been sawed open and polished on the edges to reveal quartz crystals growing inside. They were purple, like amethysts, and were quite a success. But as Griffin began to speak at some length of metamorphic rock and such scientific things, his audience's eyes glazed.

"Did you bring back any weapons, milord?" Mrs. Arbuthnot inquired. "I heard some rumor of a spear."

"Unfortunately, I did not bring the spear with me this evening. I have this little hunting knife," he said, bringing forth a wicked-looking knife with an ivory handle and a blade eight inches long. "It is used in the hunt, and to skin and carve the catch. Do be careful," he said, passing it along. "It is very sharp. I saw an Indian cut off a man's hand with this same knife."

Mrs. Arbuthnot emitted a squeal of delighted terror, and the knife clattered to the ground.

Details of this cruel deed were demanded. "The fellow had stolen a pot. Pots are objects of rare value with that particular tribe," he explained.

"Cut off a hand for stealing a pot?" Mrs. Arbuthnot gasped.

"One would take them for Christians," Griffin said.

The vicar ruffled up at this. "If you are referring to the precept of an eye for an eye, Griffin, you have not got it quite right."

"No, Vicar, I am referring to our precept; if thy eye scandalize thee, pluck it out, and presumably if thy hand seize what don't belong to it, cut it off." He cast a flickering glance at the duke, who paled visibly.

The knife was retrieved and passed gingerly from hand to hand, with the utmost caution.

Mrs. Arbuthnot went to the trunk and lifted out a miniature doll, with a bit of black hair attached to it. "What is this strange thing?" she asked.

"That is a *macumba* doll."

"What on earth is a *macumba*?" the lady asked.

"It is a religious cult brought from Africa by the slaves imported to Brazil. In the Caribbean they have a similar religion called voodoo. It is believed the word voodoo derives from Vodun, one of their gods."

"That is interesting," the vicar said. "Can you tell us something about this religion, Lord Griffin?"

"Only from scraps I have picked up from the natives. The language was a barrier, of course. I learned a fair bit of Tupi, a sort of lingua franca used by the missionaries, but there are many dialects. The divine beings worshiped in their religion are called *loa*. The natives believe they are inhabited by the spirit of these *loa* during religious observances, and perform dances and—er other rituals," he said discreetly. Mrs. Arbuthnot gave him a saucy smile. "They have great bonfires, usually on the beach."

"Fire often plays an integral part in primitive religions," the vicar nodded. "And water, too, of course. We use it ourselves in baptism."

"They also have some animal sacrifice, mostly chickens, in my limited experience," Griffin continued.

Myra laughed. "Chickens!"

"You forget our ancient Christian ritual of sacrificing the lamb," the vicar said, mildly repressive. "What else is in your trunk, milord?" he asked, for he knew the likelihood of argument breaking out if religion became the topic.

Griffin showed them carvings—some of them quite scandalous, of full-grown naked women with enormous breasts and men with enlarged organs. Myra averted her eyes at these specimens. Griffin also displayed weaving, native clothing, and the feathers of strange birds. He described the natives' diet and living conditions, causing a few shudders among the ladies. The guests asked random questions while the tea tray was brought in. At ten-thirty, they began making preparations to leave. Soon no guests remained except Mrs. Arbuthnot and Griffin. The lady was loath to leave. She could see as clear as day that Myra was going to jilt Griffin, and was eager to try her hand with him.

"You did not tell us about the *macumba* doll, Lord Griffin," she said, looking at the curious object.

"I did not wish to scandalize the vicar," he replied. "That is an object of revenge. When the followers of *macumba* wish to harm or even kill an enemy, they fashion a doll in the enemy's likeness." In a mischievous mood, he added, "This one was made by a fellow who was jilted by his lady. He made this image of the usurper, and added a lock of his hair. The hair you see is human. For the magic to work, there must be something belonging to the victim. The victim's enemy then sticks pins in the doll," he continued, looking not at Mrs. Arbuthnot, but at Dunsmore.

Griffin removed a pin from the doll's arm. "This, I fancy, gave the victim a lame arm. If he had stuck it here," he said, removing the pin and inserting it in the head, "he would have caused a migraine. Here"—he put the pin in the ankle—"a lame leg. And when he inserted it here," he said, plunging it into the heart, "the victim, already weakened by injuries, dies a horrible, slow death."

"What a horrid story!" Mrs. Arbuthnot exclaimed, clutching her heart. "Surely it cannot work!"

"Strangely, it does, if the victim believes. It is all in the mind, you see. I have personally seen victims wither on the vine from this very cause."

99

"But why would the victim give the doll maker a lock of his hair?" the widow asked.

"He does not give it. It is obtained by stealth. It need not be hair, incidentally. A piece of personal clothing will do, if it has touched the victim's body."

Myra shivered.

"This *macumba* is extremely powerful," he continued. "Look to your locks, ladies!"

Mrs. Arbuthnot realized she had outstayed her welcome, and took a reluctant leave. "You must call one day and tell me more about this fascinating business, Lord Griffin," she said, before leaving.

"I look forward to it, madam."

Mrs. Newbold accompanied the parting guest to the door. In the saloon, Griffin turned a steely eye on the duke and said, "Now that we are alone, at last, we can have some meaningful conversation. I think you know what I mean, Duke? Myra?"

Chapter Eleven

The duke and Myra sat huddled together for safety on the sofa. "I told you I need some time to make up my mind," Myra sulked.

From the corner of his eye, Griffin noticed Alice, sitting with her eyes like saucers and her ears on the stretch. "Leave us, Sal. This is private."

She flounced out of the room and met her mama in the hall, just returning from the door. Mrs. Newbold grumbled, "I am sorry I invited that Arbuthnot creature. She is tossing her bonnet at Griffin, certainly."

"What of it? You want Myra to marry the duke, do you not?"

"Indeed I do, but that is not to say I want to see Griffin make a misalliance. Did you see her rolling her eyes at him? And staying till the last dog was hung. No breeding." She began hurrying toward the saloon.

"Don't go in, Mama. They are getting down to brass tacks now."

The mother slapped her palms to her cheeks.

"Mercy! Thank goodness they waited till the guests had left. Mrs. Arbuthnot would have spread the story all over the village. Tell Myra I am waiting in my bedroom to hear what happens."

"I'll tell her."

Alice waited until her mother had left, then drew a chair up outside the saloon door, hidden from view of those within, and made herself comfortable to listen. She heard Griffin say, "Time is up, milady. You must fish or draw bait."

Alice felt her heart tighten to a hard ball in her chest. For a moment, no sound came from the saloon. She leaned forward in her chair to peer around the door frame. Myra sat fiddling with the ribbons on her gown. "Well, what is it to be?" Griffin demanded gruffly.

"I need a little more time."

Griffin's voice rose in frustration. "You have had two weeks!"

The duke jumped up from his chair. "Now see here, Griffin! There is no need to badger the poor girl. You can see what a state she is in." Myra began sniffling. He passed her his handkerchief.

Griffin said, "What I see is that Miss Newbold cares for no one but herself. We have been hearing of her racking indecision for long enough, but it does not prevent her from dawdling about the shops in the village. *You* may be content to drag at her heels until you are old and gray, Dunsmore. I have better things to do."

"Any gentleman who has better things to do than drag at—that is to say, to tend to the woman he loves, is not a gentleman."

Griffin's head turned slowly to cast a menacing look at his adversary. When he spoke, his voice was like ice. "Are you saying I am not a gentleman,

Dunsmore? That is a highly provocative statement."

Dunsmore, realizing what he had said, began to reverse his position. "I did not mean . . . Naturally—I mean to say—"

"If one of us is not a gentleman, I would bequeath that questionable distinction on yourself, Duke. It was you who made up to another man's fiancée during his absence, and had not even the common courtesy to withdraw your offer when the lawful fiancé returned."

"Dunsmore is not unlawful," Myra said heatedly.

"But I love her," Dunsmore said.

"So do I," Griffin said, looking from one to the other. "What do you suggest we do about it? I think we must leave it up to the lady." He went to Myra and removed the handkerchief from her fingers. She lifted her eyes to him. There was not a trace of a tear, but only a wildly triumphant excitement. Their eyes met and held. She saw the frustration in his, and the dawning knowledge. As he realized her stunt, the frustration firmed to anger.

Myra tossed her head and said, "Don't think I will marry you if you call Dunsmore out, for I shan't. You are behaving like a savage, Griffin."

Griffin's eyes slewed to the duke. "Then perhaps I shall just call him out for the fun of it. My blood lust has not been satisfied recently."

Dunsmore looked from his beloved to his tormentor, and wished he were a hundred miles away. Griffin would actually *enjoy* a duel. What chance had he against a man who killed wild boar with a spear? Griffin could break his neck with his bare hands, and enjoy it. All well and good for Myra to chastise Griffin. She was not the one who would have to face him across the "court of twelve paces."

"Can we not settle this like gentlemen?" he said in a weak voice.

A diabolical smile seized Griffin's features. "My fiancée has just told me I am not a gentleman. I am a savage—and you—" He hunched his shoulders in dismissal of Dunsmore's claim to gentility. When this did not rouse the duke to ire, he turned back to Myra. "I shall have my answer by noon tomorrow. Not a minute longer. If I do not hear from you by then, Myra, I shall assume you have come to your senses, and sent our wedding notice to the papers, in which case I shall not expect to find you here, Duke," he said, tossing a menacing glance to Dunsmore. "You understand my meaning?"

Myra looked at her protector with a fiery eye, tacitly demanding that he fight for her.

"Naturally, I shall leave if Myra does not choose me," the duke said, and escaped while he could. He was too upset to wonder what Alice was doing at the doorway.

Myra jumped up, but before following Dunsmore, she turned her wrath on Griffin. "Don't think you can bully me in this fashion, Griffin. I will not be subject to your whims."

"If you marry me, madam, you will do exactly as I say."

She felt a thrill at his strong words, and the black eyes burning into hers. Griffin heard her shallow gasps, and saw her breast heave. He saw the feverish glow in her eyes, and hoped all might not be lost yet. She had never looked more beautiful. The intensity of the moment lent a new vividness to her charms. He must have been mistaken earlier, when he thought she was only toying with him for her own vanity's sake.

"Myra, darling. You know it is me you love," he

said in ardent accents. He drew her, unprotesting, into his arms, and kissed her ruthlessly.

In the hall, Alice watched with a curious sense of detachment, as if she were at the theater. It did not seem real to her yet. Later she would assimilate the meaning of this ardent embrace, but for now, she just watched, anticipating the emptiness that would come later. At least the torment of futile hoping was over, and she could begin to forget Griffin. Myra was going to marry him. She would try to be happy for him—for them.

Myra gave herself up to the punishing kiss for as long as her senses could stand it. In the end, she did not know whether she was more afraid or thrilled, but she knew Dunny never had this effect on her.

"Oh, Griffin!" she moaned softly at his collarbone. "You will give me a little longer to make up my mind, won't you?"

The words were like a dash of ice water. He released her from his arms. She turned aside shyly, but not before he saw the sly look in her eyes. He gazed a moment at her conniving face, and was struck with the fact that her chin was a little more forward than he had ever noticed before. It was more apparent in profile.

"I am afraid not, Myra. In fact, I must know one way or the other now, tonight."

"But you said tomorrow at noon."

"Gentlemen can change their minds, too. Tell me, *now*." His voice was pitched low, but not soft or tender.

She heard the lash sting of his words, and pouted. "You must know I am too upset to think straight now, Griffin, after that mauling."

"My wife must be able to keep her head in greater perils than an embrace. Who knows what our future might hold? One encounters wilder animals than an infatuated lover in primitive countries. Lions, tigers, elephants in heat."

"But you said you would not go back to Brazil!"

"I do not intend to. You did not extract a promise from me about Africa, however."

"Africa!"

"I have not yet visited the dark continent."

"You promised you would stay home, Griffin!"

"I fear that is a promise I will not be able to fulfill. It would be unfair to misrepresent our future to you."

"If you are going to be like that, then I shan't marry you, and that's final!" she declared, and waited for him to reassure her.

Griffin shrugged his shoulders. "So be it."

She ran from the room to follow Dunsmore. Alice, her mind reeling from the sudden change in the situation, managed to say, "The duke went to the library." Myra ran after him.

"Why did you not stand up to that bully?" Myra demanded, when she ran the duke to ground in the library.

Dunsmore firmed his shoulders and regarded her with a critical eye never directed her way before. "There is much in what Griffin says, Myra. He and I look like fools, sitting on our hands while you parade us about in turn. You must make up your mind."

Myra, having just whistled one excellent parti down the wind, was not about to lose the other. "But I have made up my mind, Dunny darling. I told him, just now."

A smile trembled on his lips, all criticism forgotten. "Did you really? You mean—you have chosen me!"

"Of course I did, old silly. It was you all the time." She saw the question in his blue eyes, and added swiftly, "I just realized I could never marry him. Never! He frightens me to death."

"Me, too."

"I did not realize it until Griffin acted so horrid tonight, with all that talk of sticking pins in dolls."

Dunsmore reached for his handkerchief to wipe his beaded brow. His face froze, and he said in a hollow voice, "He's got my handkerchief! He'll kill me!"

"Whatever do you mean, Dunny?"

"I gave my handkerchief to you, and he took it. He'll make one of those dolls and stick pins in it. Oh, my God! My arm is going stiff already." He fell back against the sofa cushions and began massaging his left arm with his right hand.

"He could not possibly have made a doll already!"

"I feel pins in my fingers."

"What you have to do is prevent yourself from believing it, Dunny. If you don't believe it, it cannot hurt you."

"It is growing more numb by the minute!"

"Or you could ask for your handkerchief back."

The duke did not even bother to reply to this idea. He was in enough pain that he wanted to get upstairs to bed, before he lost the use of his legs as well.

In the hallway, Alice stood a moment, adjusting to what she had just witnessed. Disbelief and anger warred within her, untouched with euphoria. Her first anger was for Myra, but as she thought of that scene, it occurred to her that really Griffin was to blame. Myra was right; he *had* become too primitive for England. He could have carried the day, if

107

only he had behaved himself. But that was the way with Griffin. He always went that inch too far. She watched a moment as he packed up his trunk, then walked into the room. "You made a fine botch of that, Griffin," she said brusquely.

"It was high time she make up her mind."

"She had made it up. She was going to choose you, until you let your temper get away on you."

"I had ample provocation."

"If you had just said something nice, instead of scaring her with talk of lions and tigers. You never mentioned Africa before."

"One never knows what the future might bring. I do not rule Africa out. I will not have my life, and my work, circumscribed by a vain woman."

"You knew what Myra was like all along. She never hid her distaste for travel to primitive places. I used to wonder why she did not leap at the chance of marrying you, but I begin to see she is wiser than I. You *are* a primitive beast. I think you had best return to the jungle and marry Princess Nwani, for you are no longer fit for civilized society. Frightening poor Dunsmore like that—"

"The man is half woman. How can she tolerate his sniveling and simpering. He would not last a day in Brazil."

"It is extremely unlikely he will ever be in Brazil. This is England, Griffin, and you won't last long here if you do not lick yourself into shape. Your barbarism was amusing at first, but the novelty begins to wear thin. If you had behaved decently tonight, you could have won Myra back. Instead you frightened her out of her wits with that attack, you very likely gave Dunsmore a heart attack, and you lost any chance of marrying Myra. Try, if you can, to do one decent thing and speak to the duke.

Tell him you do not plan to fight a duel; you are bowing out, like the gentleman you used to be."

"Bruxa!"

"Broosha yourself!" she said angrily, and stalked from the room before the tears sprang to her eyes.

Chapter Twelve

The duke's condition worsened. The numbness flew from his left arm to his right. His original fear of having a duel forced on him was not forgotten either. If Myra chose Griffin, Dunsmore was to leave Newbold Hall, but the outcome if Myra chose himself had not been settled. A duel was by no means out of the question, even if his shooting arm had seized up on him entirely. Mrs. Newbold was of estimable help to the duke in the way of possets and embrocations. His health was her major concern, as soon as she had sent the wedding announcements in to the London papers and sent out the invitations.

For two days, not a word was heard from Griffin. It was assumed he knew of the wedding, for the announcement was also sent into the local paper. Myra and her mama were busy tending the duke in his misery, and making wedding preparations. Alice also had her duties to perform, but she found time to wonder how Griffin was taking the news.

"He has not returned to London," Alice said. "I met Nancy Warwick this morning when I was getting the liniment for Dunsmore, and she told me she had seen Griffin in the village an hour earlier."

"I daresay he was buying more pins to stick in Dunny," Myra said, with an angry toss of her curls. Now that she had definitely settled on the duke, Griffin was talked down as a positive ogre.

"Don't be so foolish," Alice scoffed.

"The doll and pins work if the victim believes, and Dunny does believe it. Do you not remember how Griffin glared at Dunny when he was telling about the man who stole another man's sweetheart? Then he grabbed Dunny's handkerchief right out of my hand. Poor Dunny is in a cold sweat, waiting for the pin to strike his heart. If Griffin thinks I will marry him after he has murdered Dunny, he will be sorely disappointed."

Alice knew the black magic art was a bag of moonshine, but as Dunsmore believed it, someone would have to make Griffin remove the curse. She was sorry she had given him such a dressing down. He might refuse to do it, to spite them all. She feared Griffin would soon sheer off to London, and wanted to see him before he left. She had her mare saddled up at once and cantered over to Mersham Abbey.

The spring weather had turned to summer. Wildflowers spangled the meadow, and the sky overhead was tinged with a pale petal pink. She was already uncomfortably warm in her riding habit. At the stable, Lafferty told her his lordship was in the conservatory, and she went in search of him.

Inside the glass-walled conservatory, it was punishingly hot. Alice unbuttoned her jacket and removed her bonnet as she moved through the rows of plants, looking for Griffin.

She found him bent over a table, at work examining specimens brought home from Brazil. His gardener had potted the seeds, and some had already sprouted. Griffin looked up and smiled to see Alice, all pink and disheveled from her ride, with a riot of curls dancing at her cheek. She did not look so very different than she had when he left five years before. At closer range, her open jacket revealed a more mature figure. He noticed that she had grown into a well-formed lady.

"Come and have a look at this, Sal," he said.

She looked at a green sprout two inches high growing out of a terra-cotta pot. It appeared to consist of one leaf, curled up in a spike. "What is it?" she asked.

"It is a banana tree, the first to sprout. In my eagerness, I planted a few on board ship on my way home. It has taken six weeks. I had nearly given up on it. Is it not marvelous?"

She blinked at the little green sprout. "Very interesting. It is not very large, is it?"

"It grows to enormous heights. I have watched seedlings sprout four to six inches a day, in ideal conditions. It must be kept moist and warm."

"Ah, what is a banana?"

"A yellow, soft pulpy fruit much admired in South America."

"Something like a peach?"

"No, no, completely different. It is actually an herb, but the plant it grows on looks like a tree, with long, flat leaves. In Bahia, they use the leaves for umbrellas, among other things. The fruit grow in enormous bunches. They look as if they are growing upside down," he said, and tried to describe them to her. "I hope to bring this specimen to fruition. It will start a new fad, I wager. And this," he said, drawing forth another pot, "is a different species. There are dozens of sorts of bananas."

"Like apples. Very interesting, Griffin, but —"

"Snow White is very fond of them. I must be sure to tell Prinny," he said, smiling at the small plant. "Why?"

"Because I gave the little brute to the prince. He hinted outrageously when I was at Carlton House. I left Snow White in London, at Mama's request. My housekeeper informed me she was wreaking havoc in the saloon. It was foolish of me to bring her home, but I hope she will be happy with her new owner. Prinny sent me a very nice letter of thanks. He was having a diamond-studded collar made up for her. She'll like that. He also sent me a jewel-encrusted snuffbox as a thank-you gift."

"You don't use snuff."

"No, but it looks well on my toilet table. Mama is hinting it would hold pins. I wager she will weasel it out of me. How is everyone at Newbold Hall?"

"That is why I have come," she said, remembering with a guilty start. Griffin could always divert her with his tales.

"Trouble in love land?" he asked with a smile that looked more satirical than heartbroken. "I read the wedding announcement in the paper."

"Yes, there is trouble, and it is all your fault."

"She is not having second thoughts!" he exclaimed.

"Oh, I am sorry, Griffin. I did not mean to get your hopes up. No, Myra is not having second thoughts. It is Dunsmore."

His features eased to an expression of relief. "Now, that surprises me," he said, chewing a smile.

Alice looked at him with the dawning of comprehension. "It is not that either. He continues infatuated. It is his arm, you see."

"What ails it?"

113

"It has gone numb. He thinks you are sticking pins in your doll."

A loud laugh erupted. "Gudgeon. Did I not make clear that some personal item belonging to the victim is necessary?"

"You took his handkerchief that he had lent to Myra. That is what put the silly notion in his head. He is truly suffering, Griffin. You must do something."

"And she is really willing to *marry* that idiot?"

"Yes, she is, and it is your own fault. It was your talking of Africa and lions and tigers that frightened her off. I begin to think you did not want to marry her."

"You wrong me, brat. I wanted to marry her more than anything in the world. It was only late that evening that I began to suspect a flaw in her. And before you leap to her defense, let me have my say. She enjoyed the acclaim of leading Dunsmore and myself about like tame pups on a leash, and would have continued to do so as long as we let her."

"I know that. I wondered that you and Dunsmore could not see it."

"I think she intended all along to have the duke. She made a May game of me, Sal. All things considered, I would say I let her off lightly."

"I agree." She sensed his regret and said, "Are you terribly sorry she chose Dunsmore?"

"Of course I am. I feel lost. It is possible to love someone, warts and all. I sometimes wonder if it is not our lovers' warts that endear them to us. A little vanity does not go entirely amiss in a beautiful lady."

For some unaccountable reason, this reply threw Alice into a temper. "In my opinion she ought to be whipped, but it is Dunsmore who is suffering. He thinks you are killing him with black magic. Yet he resists getting better, because he is afraid you plan to call him out. You must do something, Griffin. They make me read to him every morning, since Myra and Mama are busy preparing the wedding."

He smiled. "What do you read to him? I am curious to learn what occupies that man's mind. Is it fairy tales, novels?"

"It does not matter what I read. He doesn't really listen, but he is afraid to be left alone."

"But what *do* you read?"

"Books of travel, mostly," she replied vaguely. She did not want to admit that she had taken to reading about Africa, after Griffin's announcement that he planned to go there. She was already familiar with Brazil, and had a brief acquaintance with Italy and Greece. "What are you going to do? There must be some procedure to remove the curse."

"I am not a shaman. I did not put a curse on him. The man is a fool."

"He is a fool in pain, Griffin. Have some compassion. Do *something*. He won't know the difference."

"What do you suggest? Shall I don a mask and rattle a spear over him? Kill a chicken in his honor?"

She considered this a moment, then said, "Send him back his handkerchief. He believes that is the amulet you are using to put a hex on him. Tell him all is forgiven, and he is safe. Tell him you have no intention of challenging him to a duel."

Griffin observed her carefully. "You have misunderstood the nature of an amulet, Sal. It is used as a charm against evil. What have you been reading, that you hit upon that word?"

"I was trying to discover something about witchcraft, to put Dunny's mind at ease. Will you do as I ask?"

"Perhaps, if you are very nice to me," he said, in an insinuating voice.

"What do you mean?" she asked suspiciously. She could not quite trust that impish grin. It flashed into her head that Griffin was planning to set up a flirtation with her.

"I have just lost my girl, Sal. I still need a wife." Her heart banged against her ribs, and her breaths came in shallow gasps. If he mentioned a marriage of convenience, she would hit him.

"I have been out of the country for five years. I am not familiar with the new crop of debs. Which of them would suit my purpose? A wife of good character and breeding, not an antidote, and not a Bath miss who will balk at a little travel. I don't mean to leave my lady behind for society to amuse, in those ways that society knows so well."

Her breathing resumed its steady pace. "I cannot think of any lady who would like to go to Africa," she said.

"I have no intention of going to Africa. That was just a stick to frighten Myra. You know my destination—Greece."

"And Italy?"

"And Italy, to repay my wife for clambering over the cliffs of Greece, gathering rosebuds, and whatever else we find growing there. Mama mentioned Lady Sara Winsley."

"Oh," she said. It was a sigh of regret. "She is charming, Griffin. Just the sort you would like."

"My mind is not quite made up. I want to get to know other ladies as well."

"Then allow me to mention my own special friend, Miss Sutton."

"Let us include a third. Like Paris, I shall have a choice of three ladies for the golden apple—or do I mean banana—of my title. We require a Venus, as

116

well as a Hera and Athena. God, what a conceited ass I am."

"Yes, aren't you?" she replied tartly. "I begin to wonder if I am doing Miss Sutton a favor by including her in your chosen three."

"Thus far, we have only selected two." His lips quirked in a pensive smile. "But our wits have gone begging. *You* must be the third, Sal. Athena, Goddess of wisdom."

"At least you spared me the inanity of calling me Venus. I am afraid I must decline the honor, Griffin. We are not going to London for another two weeks. Mama wants to be there a few days before the wedding, but several of the guests will be returning here with us after, and there are all sorts of arrangements to be made."

"Pity," he said.

"You won't have any trouble finding a third lady willing to make a fool of herself over you. I am not interested." She rose and said sternly, "You will do as I ask about Dunsmore?"

"If you will wait a moment, I shall get the wicked handkerchief and write a note for you to take back with you. Come in and have a chat with Mama. She is having a tea party this afternoon."

"I would prefer to wait here. I am not dressed for a tea party."

"She won't mind."

"I am in a hurry, Griffin. Would you just get the handkerchief and write the note, please." She had not meant to speak so sharply, but her nerves were stretched taut. Her visit had been a seasaw of emotion, from pity for Griffin to hope, to disappointment, and ultimately to anger.

"Bruxa!" he scowled, and left.

Alice strolled through the conservatory, telling herself she did not care a hoot if he did marry Lady

Sara or Sukey Sutton. She could take no more of this emotional hammering. Let him go to London, and let some other ladies make fools of themselves over him.

He was soon back, with the laundered handkerchief and a note. "Wish Myra well for me, and tell her I am sorry."

"Are you sorry, Griffin?" she asked, wondering if his cavalier attitude was a show to cover his pain.

"I am sorry I wasted so long mooning after her. And I am sorry you will not be one of my three potential brides."

"I prefer a gentleman who knows what he wants. You have just been put through the ordeal of being one of two waiting to learn his fate, Griffin. How can you put three ladies through the same thing? I think it is horrid and vain of you."

"It was not a public exhibition I had in mind. When a gent is on the lookout for a bride, he does not usually limit himself to one. He looks over the whole field. I have scanned the field. At least I was in London for a part of the Season, and saw the debs. I like Lady Sara. I also like your friend, Miss Sutton. I only want to get to know them a little better."

"And your third?"

"I already know you pretty well. Don't think you shall escape consideration only because you despise me."

"I do not despise you. It is just that—" There was too much to say, and as most of it could not be said to Griffin, she did not say anything, but just put the handkerchief and letter in her pocket and left.

Dunsmore was vastly relieved to receive them. The numbness fell from him like a charm. He found himself able to write a note in reply, in which he foolishly expressed the hope that he would see Griffin soon.

Chapter Thirteen

The duke had two days in which to recuperate before Griffin came calling at Newbold Hall. The visit's razor edge of terror was dulled by the presence of Lady Griffin, who accompanied her son. It was felt that Griffin would have left his mama at home if he had come to create a new quarrel. Naturally Lady Griffin was curious to see what marvel of manlihood had superceded Griffin in Myra's affections.

The first glance told her looks were not the duke's long suit. A very few moments of his conversation told her the man was no mental giant either, although he managed to thank her for her congratulations three or four times, and tell her he felt himself the most fortunate man on earth.

"Where will you be going for your wedding trip?" Lady Griffin inquired, more for politeness's sake than from curiosity.

"A jaunt to Brighton, perhaps, until I recuperate."

"I was so sorry to hear about your arm. Griffin

mentioned the misunderstanding to me. You must pay no heed to those foolish witchcraft tales my son tells. And after you recuperate, will you go abroad? The half of England is in Paris, since we have rooted Boney."

"We Dunsmores are not much for travel. We are bracing ourselves for the trip to Scotland for Myra to meet the folks, then it will be back to London for us. The Dunsmores have always been active in the House. The Corn Laws are my own special concern."

Lady Griffin mentally translated this to mean he would be running after more profitable sinecures. This had always been the Dunsmores main activity in the House. It occurred to her that James might avail himself of some of this easy money, and she said to her son, "You might think of taking your seat, too, James."

Dunsmore tried to conceal his horror at this awful possibility. "I have no doubt your expertise would be invaluable in thrashing out the Corn Laws, Griffin," he said in a strained voice. "Where would you stand when you take your seat?"

A smile quirked Griffin's lips. "On the side of the angels, Dunsmore."

"Ah. I knew you was still a Christian. Your mama just mentioned it, but I meant vis-à-vis the Corn Laws."

"I am a Whig. I would be in favor of lowering the tariffs, or removing them entirely."

Dunsmore stared at such heresy. "But you have no idea how the price of wheat had fallen! Down from a hundred and seventeen shillings the bushel to sixty-nine, in one year. We only set the price at eighty shillings."

"Only gave yourselves a present of eleven shillings on each bushel, on the backs of the starving public. Magnanimous! I have not heard there was any outcry in Parliament to lower the price when it reached that ridiculous hundred and seventeen shillings."

"Yes, but most of us in the House are landowners, you see. It would come out of our own pockets."

Griffin was shocked at such simple veracity coming from a politician. "I trust Liverpool does not send you out on the hustings, Dunsmore."

"Eh? What do you mean by that? Are you suggesting I am disloyal to the Tories?"

"No, Dunsmore. I think you are a perfect model of a Tory."

Dunsmore smiled at this imagined compliment, until he noticed the sneer growing on Griffin's lips. "Ah, I understand you now. You are a Whig. Forgot. Heh heh. I am always willing to hear both sides. If you have something on your mind about these Corn Laws, I wish you would get it off your chest."

"I just did."

This lockjaw conversation continued for five minutes, by which time Lady Griffin had taken Dunsmore's measure and was ready to discuss more interesting things than the price of food. "Gentlemen, please! No politics. Remember there are ladies present. And I hope these same ladies, along with the duke, of course, will all come to me tomorrow evening for dinner."

"Oh no, we cannot," Myra said at once. She had been on thorns when Griffin turned satirical. She knew perfectly well he was still in love with her, because he had hardly trusted himself to look at her since entering. He was up to some mischief, trying to get Dunny to Mersham to put another curse on him.

Mrs. Newbold tried to put a good face on her

daughter's blunt refusal. "We are invited out to-morrow evening, Lady Griffin," she explained un-truthfully.

"Pity. Do you think you might spare me Alice at least? Griffin has some young people coming down from London for a few days. Your special friend, Miss Sutton, is among them, Alice."

Alice's eyes flew to Griffin, who cocked his head and smiled innocently. Mrs. Newbold gave Alice her permission to skip the imaginary dinner party.

"You mentioned young people, Lady Griffin," Alice said. "Would I know the other guests?"

"I daresay you have heard me speak of Lady Sara Winsley, old Lord Calmet's daughter. She is my goddaughter."

"Of course." Her eyes moved to Griffin. "That sounds like a sad surfeit of ladies," she said.

"Personally I think three to one the proper ratio, but Mama will invite a few local gentlemen to round off the parties she has planned."

"The idiot actually expected me to host a party for ladies only." Lady Griffin laughed.

"Perhaps he was afraid of the competition, ma'am," Alice said.

"Aye, his hide is tender after losing Myra. We were sorry to hear of your decision, my dear," she said to Myra, "but of course the dear duke is charming. I know you will both be very happy to-gether. I cannot think of anyone who would suit you better."

Myra smiled and blushed at this barbed compli-ment, and explained at quite unnecessary length that she had the highest regard for Griffin, but Dunsmore had just swept her off her feet. Lady Griffin nodded in contemplation, wondering that Dunsmore could even lift a broom, much less put it to such effect.

Alice seized the opportunity to quiz Griffin about his visitors. "I understood you would be going to London to do your courting. Why did you change your mind?"

"You recall my insistence on three competitors for my golden banana? You refused to go to London. It was a case of delivering the mountain to Mohamet."

"I am sure you could have found another lady to complete your trio in London."

"Very likely, but I wanted you. I always feel more at home amid the world of flora, fur, and feathers. I am not a saloon-ish sort of person. Then, too, after a little consideration, I realized the masculine competition was thinner here."

"Are you cultivating modesty as a part of your bag of tricks, Griffin? I suggest you stick to your usual masculine arrogance."

He bowed. "Whatever you say. You do appreciate my combining humble agreement with an arrogant disregard of your suggestion?" he added. Laughter danced in his dark eyes.

"I believe it is called hypocrisy."

"A Newbold lady ought to appreciate that," he retorted.

The sting in his words annoyed her. It even occurred to her that Griffin was trying to repay Myra through her. Alice resented that she had been maneuvered into taking part in Griffin's marital contest, yet she admitted she would have been devastated had she been left out.

Lady Griffin began to collect her reticule, and soon the guests left. Myra and her mama discussed the visit at some length.

"Griffin seems to be taking it well," Mrs. Newbold was so unwise as to say.

Myra had to straighten her out on that score.

"He was full of mischief. Did you not hear him baiting Dunny? He was very upset, but trying to hide it. His pride, you know. Griffin always had a deal of pride. He is trying to assuage his grief by filling his house with girls, to make me jealous. Alice will tell us how he behaves. He invited her so she would run home to me with all the details. As if I care a hoot."

Alice, listening, thought there might be a soupçon of truth in what her sister said. Griffin was not taking his rejection so well as he pretended. That angry slur about Myra's hypocrisy revealed a lingering rancor.

Alice went up to her room to plan how to outshine Lady Sara and Sukey Sutton. Griffin would have more than a dinner party to entertain them. There would be routs and riding and perhaps even a ball over the next few days. Lady Sara and Sukey would be at Mersham twenty-four hours a day, working their charms on Griffin, while she would only be there on those more formal occasions when she was invited. Tomorrow evening she would see how Griffin behaved with all his ladies.

The Newbolds had no invitation for the next evening, but they were, in fact, dining out that evening. Alice made her toilette and went with them. The evening seemed to last forever, and during the whole four hours, she scarcely thought of anything but Griffin's house party. She wondered when Lady Sara and Sukey were arriving. London was not far. They might be there for lunch, and have a whole afternoon's head start on winning Griffin.

She was put out of her misery the next morning. Mrs. Newbold received a note from Lady Griffin, asking if she could spare Alice to her for a few days, to help entertain Griffin's guests. Mrs. Newbold, she was sure, realized the delicacy of the situation. Griffin would feel uncomfortable calling at Newbold to pick Alice up for all the pending outings. And since Sukey Sutton was a special friend of Alice, she made sure the girls would like to be together. She mentioned what clothing would be useful, and suggested Alice have her mount sent to Mersham as well.

Mrs. Newbold read the letter to Alice, fully expecting the girl to set her jaw against the plan. "A nuisance for you, when we have the duke here, but I do wish you would go along with it, Sal. It will keep Griffin from pouncing in on us every time we turn around."

Alice could scarcely believe her luck. She hid her pleasure, for she did not want her mama to suspect her feelings for Griffin.

"If you think it will help, Mama, I have no objection. I should like to spend some time with Sukey."

"That is exactly who you *will* spend your time with. I wager Lady Griffin has already arranged a match between Griffin and Lady Sara. This is a pretext for them to get to know each other better. She would not want Lady Sara to come alone. It would look so very particular, especially if something comes up to scotch the match. There is no saying with Griffin. The lad has some odd kicks in his gallop. He will drag poor Lady Sara off to Africa to be eaten alive by cannonballs."

Alice agreed, yet it was those odd kicks that she particularly liked in him. He was a little different from other men—more adventurous, more dashing. She hurried off to begin choosing outfits to take to Mersham.

Chapter Fourteen

No specific hour had been set for Alice's arrival. She did not want to appear eager and arrive too early, yet she did not want to miss a minute of the fun. Myra took the visit in dislike, and was disgruntled all morning.

"He has a lot of gall, expecting Alice to entertain his guests for him. Dunny and I wanted her to drive out with us this afternoon."

"Yes, by Jove, if you are to entertain anyone, you ought to entertain us," Dunsmore said supportively, then bit his lip when his beloved glared at him.

"We do not need entertaining, Dunny," Myra told him. "We can entertain ourselves. We shall drive past Mersham and watch for Lady Sara's arrival."

"I would not give him the satisfaction," Mrs. Newbold said.

She was beginning to get the awful idea that Myra regretted her choice. It was imperative to remove her from Griffin's ken at once. "What we ought to do is return to London. There are a hundred things I could be doing there, and you, too,

Duke. I daresay you ought to be doing something about those Corn Laws you are always talking about."

"By Jove!" he exclaimed eagerly, though it was not the Corn Laws that urged him to London. He would have been as happy to go to Brighton, or Bath, or anywhere that Griffin was not.

"Oh, do let us go!" Myra exclaimed. "I cannot think why we ever came home in the first place."

"What about me?" Alice asked in alarm, seeing the visit to Mersham fade before her very eyes.

"You go to Griffin's party, and hitch a drive back to London with Miss Sutton when the party is over," Mrs. Newbold said. "You will know by then if Griffin offered for Lady Sara." A quick peep told her Myra's cheeks did not blanch at the idea of some other lady nabbing Griffin. It was just pique and boredom that ailed her.

It was finally settled that Alice would go to Mersham at five o'clock, arriving in time to make her toilette for the evening. As Newbold was all abustle with packing and canceling social engagements, she could not get away earlier.

Her mama said, "Be sure you say we are leaving tomorrow morning, Sal, for I told Lady Griffin we are dining out this evening. If she asks, but she won't, tell her we are dining with our cousins at Headcorn. She does not visit them; she will never know the difference."

It chanced that Alice arrived at the same hour as her friend, Miss Sutton, and her mama, who was chaperoning her. The girls greeted each other enthusiastically at the doorway before entering. Sukey had taken terrific pains with her toilette. Rice powder bleached the smattering of freckles across her nose. She had had her red curls cut *à la victime*, and looked quite ravishing in a new pomona green traveling suit.

"I could not believe my eyes when Mama received the note, for we scarcely know the Griffins," she said to Alice. "I know this was your doing. Thank you ever so much. London was all abuzz when Myra's engagement to the duke was announced. Everyone hoped Griffin would return to town, but this is much better. Is Lady Sara here yet?"

"I have no idea. I just arrived myself. The greatest luck, Sukey. Lady Griffin has invited me to stay here for the whole party."

Mrs. Sutton, a handsome lady who gave some idea how her daughter would look in twenty years, called the girls to order and took them inside, where Griffin and Lady Sara awaited them. The cunning Lady Sara had arrived before luncheon, and was already familiar with the running of the household. At five and twenty, she did not feel the necessity of a chaperone for a visit to her godmother's house.

She was a tall brunet, rather in Lady Griffin's own style, but cleverer, and with considerably more town bronze. She fancied herself a trifle "blue," which, perhaps, accounted for her still being on the shelf at a quarter of a century.

She greeted the new arrivals graciously. "Lady Griffin has just gone abovestairs to begin her toilette. I shall play hostess for Griffin. Allow me to welcome you to Mersham, ladies," she said, with a proprietary gleam in her handsome green eyes. "You will want to freshen up before having a glass of sherry. You are in the blue suite, Mrs. Sutton. A delightful room, with Chinese wallpaper. And you, Sukey, are next door. We have put you in the same wing, Alice, for I know you two giddy girls will

129

want to be close to each other. You are just across the hall from Sukey. I shall give you the grand tour tomorrow morning."

"I have known Mersham Abbey forever," Alice replied in confusion.

"Welcome to Mersham," Griffin said, shaking the ladies' hands. He even shook Alice's, which she found rather odd. She sensed that he was ill at ease in his role as host. Having left England at a young age, he was not completely familiar with his duties.

The new guests went upstairs, where they made short shrift of washing up. "Has she had an offer from him already?" Mrs. Sutton snorted. "One would think so, to judge by her forthcoming manner."

"She always pushes too hard," Sukey explained. "That is the only reason she has not nabbed a fellow yet, for she is very pretty and has a huge fortune."

"Griffin is not interested in the blunt, or he would not have offered for Myra Newbold," Mrs. Sutton said. "No offense, Alice. I consider you quite as another daughter."

"No, Griffin is not a fortune hunter," Alice assured them.

The ladies were back downstairs before the cat could shake its tail. Lady Sara, sitting beside Griffin on the sofa and admiring his South American trophies to the top of her bent, expressed astonishment at the speed of their return.

"Did the servants not put water in your rooms? Fie, Griffin," she said with a playful tap on his wrist, "your servants are falling into bad habits."

"There was plenty of water," Mrs. Sutton said. "As we will be changing for dinner so soon, we did not see the need of a bath."

"Would you like tea or wine, ma'am?" Griffin asked.

"The Madeira is excellent," Lady Sara said, lifting a glass and sipping. "It is a wonderfully passionate wine. Papa has some of this same vintage put down. It will last a hundred and fifty years. Imagine!"

Mrs. Sutton asked for sherry. Sherry was poured, and the group settled in for some chat. Lady Sara had ascertained the schedule of pending events, and enumerated them for the guests. "A quiet evening tonight, as you will all be tired from travel. We thought some riding tomorrow morning, and perhaps a trip into Headcorn in the afternoon for the girls to see the shops. Griffin has arranged a rout for the evening."

"I did not bring my mount!" Sukey exclaimed.

Lady Sara laughed gaily. "I fear you are out of luck if you expect to borrow one from Griffin. His stalls are to let."

"Perhaps the Newbolds could oblige you," Griffin suggested, looking at Alice.

"Yes, Mama's mount is standing idle. Why do you not ask the groom to have it sent over for Sukey's use, Griffin?"

"I hope it is a gentle goer," Lady Sara said, feigning concern. "As I recall, Sukey, you are not exactly a bruising rider. Did you hurt yourself badly in that tumble the other day in Rotten Row?"

"I did not tumble," Sukey said. "I just slipped a little. The saddle was put on loosely."

"You should always check that before mounting," Lady Sara told her.

"It is a lady's mount. Sukey will have no trouble," Alice said.

They were the last words she spoke for several minutes. She had only known Lady Sara for a month. She had always taken her for an obliging sort of lady. She sensed the change in her now, and soon realized that it was a determination to win Griffin that accounted for it. Little slurs on Sukey and herself were introduced needlessly into the conversation, and much was made of the long friendship between the Calmets and the Griffins. It was all done with a grace and seeming concern that might fool the unwary, but it did not fool Alice or the Suttons.

Lady Griffin appeared. Lady Sara rose and embraced her. "Dear Godmama. What a lovely visit this is. I wish I saw more of you, but you never come to London."

"It was kind of your mama to spare you to me."

After a short visit, the guests went abovestairs to change for dinner. "I expect Sara will be dripping in diamonds when she dresses for evening," Sukey said angrily, as she left Alice at her door.

Lady Griffin supplied maids to assist the girls in their toilettes. White was not necessary at a country party, and Alice wore a simple jonquil gown, whose main adornment was a ruched hem held up with green ribbons. She wore her pearls and meant to carry a fan, but she forgot it in her room. Sukey, feeling a visit at a noble house was as formal as London, wore white, which was not her most flattering color. They were surprised to see they had beat Lady Sara to the saloon. Lady Griffin and her son were there, however, and paid them some pretty compliments on their looks.

It was ten minutes before Lady Sara made her grand entrance. Both girls knew at a glance that they were outshone by her diamonds and even more by her low-cut dark green gown. She held her dark head high, and looked as regal as a queen. It did not take a genius to see Griffin was bowled over by her. A spontaneous smile grew on his lips as he studied her.

Lady Sara paused at the doorway and made a moue in Griffin's direction. "Silly me!" she exclaimed. "I am overdressed. So vulgar of me. Pay me no heed." She swayed in, with every eye glued on her white bosoms and shapely form. "I meant my toilette as a compliment to Mersham. One does feel, when she visits one of the finest historical homes in England, that she owes it her best effort."

Griffin rose and bowed. "On behalf of Mersham, may I express my appreciation, Sara."

As their eyes met, the very air seemed to crackle with excitement. Alice and Sukey exchanged a defeated look.

Lady Griffin had been a beauty herself in her day, and recognized all the tricks. She had been annoyed with her son for falling in love with that dull clod of a Myra Newbold. She now realized that she did not want him offering for this show-off either.

She said, "Mersham is most famous for its gardens, Sara. Perhaps you should go out and make your curtsy to the flowers." Her voice was polite, even merry. Only her son recognized her feelings, and gave her a quizzing look.

Lady Sara took this up immediately. "And what divine flowers they are, Lady Griffin. You must let me take some cuttings home. I have never seen anything as beautiful as that Griffin Rose. Our gardener would be green with envy."

Lady Griffin was mollified by this blatant flattery, and condescended to discuss the roses until dinner was called. The table was lopsided with five ladies and only one gentleman, but the conversation never flagged. Lady Sara encouraged Griffin to horrify them with Brazilian tales, and kept up her end by relaying the latest gossip from London.

The group was small and informal enough that Griffin did not bother with the farce of staying behind for a glass of port all by himself at dinner's end.

"Bring the bottle in with you, Griffin," Lady Sara suggested. "I don't see why the gentlemen should keep the good things to themselves. We ladies might like a glass of port, too. What do you say, ladies?"

"Port gives me the megrims," Lady Griffin said, "but by all means have a glass, if you are particularly fond of wine, Lady Sara."

Lady Sara recognized the need of more garden talk, and gave Griffin over to the younger ladies, as soon as she had complimented him on his port. "Excellent! This is obviously from Douro. It is so strong and red and sweet."

In the saloon, Mrs. Sutton joined Lady Sara and her hostess, to give the young girls a chance with Griffin. She was unsure at first whether Lady Sara was discussing history or flowers. The names of monarchs—Tudors and Bonnie Prince Charlie and Queen Anne flew about her head like bats at twilight. As Queen Anne had obviously not been prone to black spot, she soon realized they were talking about roses.

"I have no opinion of copper sulfate as a spray for black mold," Lady Sara proclaimed.

"That surprises me. You usually have an opinion about everything," Mrs. Sutton said demurely.

Lady Griffin flashed an appreciative glance at her. "What does your mama use, Sara?" she asked.

Across the room, Griffin tried gamely to entertain the youngsters, but he found his attention kept traveling to Sara. He recognized her for a dasher, and the change from Myra was exactly what he wanted at that time.

When the tea tray was brought in, Lady Griffin had been buttered up to the point of asking Lady Sara to take charge of the pot. There was no denying Sara had countenance. She would do any husband proud, and likely she would quit trying so hard to impress after she had landed her mate. She was intelligent, lively, certainly quite beautiful, and very keen on the gardens. That was important in the mistress of Mersham.

A short while later, Mr. Montgomery was added to the party. His punishment was nearing its end. Lady Griffin had invited him to several of the little dos she and James had arranged for the girls' visit.

Lady Sara soon had him pigeonholed. He was of no importance, unless Griffin should die on one of his foreign expeditions before producing an heir. Bearing this in mind, she was polite to Monty. Everyone else ignored him. His presence was not of sufficient interest to lend light to an evening that was rapidly sliding into tedium. Alice felt sorry for him, and after a while, she joined him in his corner.

During a lull, Lady Sara said, "May I be very bold, Lady Griffin, and suggest that we have some music? I wager these young ladies are bursting with talent. Sukey, I have heard you play before, have I not?"

"I do not play well enough to perform in public," Sukey said. "Alice can chord."

Lady Sara allowed a little laugh to escape. She feared none of these people realized she was an accomplished pianist. She disliked to put herself forward, but was eager to display her skills.

"Sukey is a fair to middling singer," her mother said. "Why do you not play for us, Lady Sara, and perhaps the girls will sing along with you?"

"I am afraid I am useless as an accompanist, Mrs. Sutton. I play mostly Schubert, and, of course,

135

the lyrics are all in German. Unless Miss Sutton and Miss Newbold know German? No? Pity. Schubert quite dotes on Goethe, you must know. His best songs were inspired by Goethe's poems. *Rastlose Liebe, Erlkönig, Meerestille,*" she said, giving them the full German pronunciation. "Would you like to tackle it, girls? The words are written down—in German."

The girls wisely declined.

"I shall certainly translate them as soon as I find a moment free," Lady Sara promised. "So many girls nowadays do not bother learning German. Odd, when our royal house is German. Indeed, old King George II hardly spoke a word of English."

"I should like to hear Schubert," Griffin said, right on cue. "I have fallen behind the times while I was away."

"So have I, and I was right here," his mama added in confusion.

"Sounds deuced interesting," Monty declared, and the matter was settled.

Griffin led Lady Sara to the music room, with the others following behind. Alice watched with a worm of discontent curling inside her, noticing how Griffin put his arm around Sara's waist. Sara smiled up at him, and he smiled back in an intimate way. They really looked remarkably handsome together. Sara suited him much better than Myra did. But, of course, she must not tell Myra that.

Lady Sara's music was already laid out on the pianoforte in preparation for her performance. She had not wasted a moment of her afternoon. The audience took seats; Lady Sara arranged a candelabrum beside her. Candlelight flickered alluringly on her white arms, and cast her gown into shining hillocks with dark shadows. She gracefully arched her wrists, and Schubert's gold cords filled the room. She played with great skill, never hitting a wrong note. At the end of each piece, there was a scatter of applause. When it died down, she would announce her next selection. No one could make heads or tails of the German words, but they were very impressed.

Monty and Griffin nodded and exchanged smiles. The ladies sat morosely, knowing they had been eclipsed entirely. When Lady Sara had performed three selections, she had reached the end of her repertoire. Griffin applauded loudly and asked for more. Instead, she demurely said she did not wish to hog the instrument, and Alice must chord for them now.

Alice went with a very poor grace and began to chord the simpler country tunes. The other younger people stood around the piano and sang, while Mrs. Sutton and Lady Griffin slipped away for a chat. After half an hour, Alice was still playing away, with no sign of fatigue. When they were all tired and happy, they went back to the morning parlor for a late-night snack.

Lady Sara enlightened them as to the latest modes in music—romantic music was the new thing. She spoke authoritatively of harmony and modulation, of melodic stimulus and marvelously graphic images, till everyone was thoroughly confused, and tired, and ready for bed. Monty left, and Griffin accompanied the ladies to the staircase.

When the others began their ascent, Lady Sara turned to Griffin and said, "I believe I left my fan at the piano. Would you come with me, Griffin? I fear the servants will have extinguished the lights, and I am afraid of the dark. Silly of me, but there you are. I want a man to lean on."

Griffin agreed immediately, and they walked off together. Alice looked down over her shoulder. The last thing she saw was Griffin and Sara, heading down the dark hall together.

"I wager he will kiss her," Sukey said angrily.

"It won't be for lack of her trying if he don't," her mama snipped.

"I shouldn't be at all surprised," Alice agreed blandly. She was accustomed to hiding her hurt, but her heart ached badly at the image Sukey's words called up.

Chapter Fifteen

Sukey Sutton tapped at Alice's door the next morning at eight o'clock. She was happy to find her friend already up and dressed in her riding habit. "Is it too early to go belowstairs?" Sukey asked uncertainly. "I have never stayed at an abbey before."

"We may be the first ones down, but breakfast will be ready," Alice assured her.

The young ladies made a pretty picture as they entered the breakfast parlor: Alice with her dark hair and plum-colored riding habit, Sukey with her red hair and green outfit, both with eager smiles. Unfortunately, there was no one to admire them except a footman.

"Are we the first ones up?" Alice asked him.

"No, Miss Newbold. His lordship and Lady Sara were up an hour ago, and have gone for a ride." Alice and Sukey exchanged an angry look. "His lordship left a note for you." The footman pointed to the table, where a folded sheet of paper sat beside one of the places.

Alice picked it up and glanced at a carelessly

scrawled two lines. 'Sal, Sara and I have ridden to Headcorn. Your mama's mount is in my stable for Miss Sutton's use. Mama will provide a groom to accompany you. Till later, G.' She showed the note to Sukey.

"She must have got up at the crack of dawn," Sukey scolded.

"And gone to Headcorn. I daresay that means she will take Griffin somewhere else this afternoon, while we are driven to the village."

They heaped their plates and enjoyed a good grumble over breakfast. Lady Sara's overbearing ways, her gowns, and her looks were subjected to vivid dissection while they ate.

"At least he remembered to send for Mama's mount," Alice said, as they drank their coffee. "Would you like to go for a ride?"

"I suppose so. Where shall we go?"

"Let us ride over to Newbold Hall. You have never seen where I live. Or we can tour the gardens here. They are famous. I expect Lady Griffin will arrange a guided tour of them some time or other."

It was agreed that they would ride to Newbold Hall and be back for lunch. Mrs. Sutton and Lady Griffin came down before they left, and approved their outing, so long as they were accompanied by a groom. The little trip gave the pleasure of an intimate coze, but it was not the sort of morning the girls had anticipated.

Over lunch, Lady Sara complimented Lady Griffin on the many excellencies of Headcorn. "I asked Griffin to take me to call on the vicar, who is a connection of Mama's. But you know that, Lady Griffin. It was your kind intercession that got him the living. He gave us a tour of that wonderful old Norman church. What a history lesson is carved there in stone. Odd to think those pagan barbarian Normans were eventually civilized enough to accept Christianity, and build those marvelous structures. It makes one feel so—Griffin calls it *saudades*. A sort of nostalgia. As we were finished early, we had a stroll around town. There was not a sign of those sleepyheads," she said, smiling indulgently at Alice and Sukey.

"I thought it was agreed we would go to Headcorn this afternoon," Mrs. Sutton reminded her.

"You will not be deprived of your outing," Lady Sara smiled. "You can chaperon the girls, Mrs. Sutton. I simply *must* have my ride. My mount gets very fidgety if she is not exercised regularly. I am afraid I spoil myself, where my mount is concerned. I will ride only the best. Griffin tells me Minerva is a man's mount, but I like a strong goer."

Lady Griffin did not care very much where they all went, so long as they left her in peace. "Leave tomorrow morning open for a tour of the garden" was all she said.

The afternoon was as frustrating as the morning. Once again, Lady Sara had finessed them. Griffin rode with her, while the others made the compulsory trip to see the church, the Beult River, and the shops. As the sights were so few, Alice took the Suttons to meet her friend, Miss Warwick, who served them a glass of wine and the latest gossip.

"Who was the lady Griffin brought to Headcorn this morning? She is beautiful. Everyone says they are engaged, for she was holding on to his arm and laughing and looking at him in the most meaningful way."

"That is Lady Sara Winsley, Lord Calmet's daughter," Alice replied, "and they are not engaged."

"I wager they soon will be. Do you know, Sal, she

141

asked him to help her select a pair of silk stockings at the drapery shop? She bought a bronze color, saying it would match Griffin's complexion. We all thought it was pretty fast, but, of course, she is a lady. I went over to buy pins when I saw them go in. Everyone was staring at them. What a handsome couple they make. I got my invitation to the rout party at Mersham this evening," she said. "I can hardly wait to see Lady Sara dance with Griffin."

By the time the carriage returned to Mersham, the ladies had achieved such a pitch of annoyance that Mrs. Sutton was speaking of writing herself a letter calling herself back to London on urgent business. Alice added that she would go with her, as her mama had told her to ride to town with the Suttons.

Lady Griffin had some tea served as soon as they returned. Lady Sara and Griffin were once again absent. The ladies bristled in vexation and tried to smile.

"Where is Lady Sara, ma'am?" Alice asked.

"She is in the garden, haranguing my gardener into giving her some cuttings. Griffin will be joining us. He is in his conservatory. You know how he dotes on his plants."

He arrived a moment later, so full of compliments and merriment that the Suttons forgave him all. He told them about giving Snow White to the prince, and showed them the letter and snuffbox. He inquired with seeming interest for Miss Sutton's success in riding Mrs. Newbold's mount, and reminded her she must save him a dance at the evening's rout.

As soon as tea was over, he excused himself and left. Alice followed him, to make sure he was not slipping out to the garden to meet Lady Sara. She caught him just as he was about to enter his conservatory. "May I have a word with you, Griffin?" she asked.

"Of course. What is it, Sal?" He opened the door, and she preceded him into the greenhouse.

She waited until the door was closed, then put her hands on her hips and lit into him. "What do you think you are doing?" she demanded fiercely.

"I was about to check my bananas. They must be kept moist."

"I am not talking about your demmed bananas. You have been ignoring all of your guests except one."

It was not necessary for him to inquire which one. "I just had tea with the Suttons," he pointed out.

"Half an hour of sipping tea does not make up for twenty-four hours of neglect. Plans were made for us to ride this morning, and go to Headcorn this afternoon. You ought to have been part of the group, and not Lady Sara's particular escort. If it was only her you wanted to see, you ought not to have invited the others."

A telltale flush around his neck revealed his lack of ease at his recent behavior. "Where were you this morning? We waited half an hour."

"We were down by eight. No one ever stirs before that at a house party. You must have left at the crack of dawn."

"The day was so fine, we decided to go on without you. Lady Sara was particularly eager to have a visit with the vicar."

"The buzz in the village is not about visiting the vicar, but about her hanging on your arm while you helped her select silk stockings, to match your complexion."

"I thought you were above listening to common gossip, Alice," he said, trying for a note of hauteur.

"No one is above listening to gossip, and don't deny the story, for I had it of—of a girl who actually saw you, making a cake of yourself."

"Sara tore her stockings on the step of my curricle. Naturally I had to replace them. Were it not for that, we would have been home sooner. It is not as though Miss Sutton was left alone. She had you."

"She did not come here to see *me*," she said angrily.

"You are the one who suggested I invite her," he said, his voice rising. He was thoroughly ashamed of himself; he knew perfectly well he had been negligent of his guests, and tried to cover his shame with a bluster of anger.

"If I had known you had already settled on Lady Sara, I would not have suggested it. You are the one who wanted to become friendly with more than one lady. Well, you have not done it. You have spent ninety-nine percent of your time chasing after Lady Sara, in the most vulgar and common way, and insulted my particular friend into the bargain."

"There is nothing vulgar or common about Sara."

"I did not say there was, though, in fact, she is goading you on, and she is plenty old enough to know better. Having a gentleman select her stockings may or may not be vulgar; it is certainly fast. If she were a real lady, she would not try to monopolize your time at the expense of your other guests."

"This is something new," he said, with a snide grin. "A Newbold giving lessons in propriety. Now that I have recovered the use of my wits, I realize Myra's display was the height of vulgarity. I did not hear you castigate *her*."

"No, for doing it in public would be vulgar as

well. You may be sure I rang many a peel over her when we were in private. Don't try to saddle me with Myra's behavior, Griffin. And furthermore," she said, working herself into a fine rant, "I fail to see how you could not get a letter to her in five years. She waited longer than you deserved. The only pity is that she had not married the duke before you came home."

"Or failing that, that she could not make up her mind without dragging the duke and myself about London like the conquests of a Roman emperor."

"A grown man cannot be dragged by a lady against his will. Myra behaved badly; you and the duke abetted her. You cannot blame this present show of bad manners on her. It is your own doing. I expect you to stand up with Miss Sutton this evening, Griffin, and Miss Warwick, from Headcorn, and any other neighbors you have invited here to watch you and Lady Sara perform."

Griffin had mentally admitted his guilt, and taken the decision to be a better host, but he was not the sort to publicly admit to a fault. With his decision made, he was able to put that at the back of his mind and concentrate on other things. He noticed the sparkle in Alice's eyes, and how pink her cheeks were. He was still half accustomed to think of her as a child, but that peel she had just rung over him held the air of authority. She had grown into a beautiful and decisive woman.

"You forgot yourself, Alice. Am I not ordered to stand up with you as well?" he said, in a joking spirit.

"I am a little particular about my partners," she replied, and flounced from the conservatory.

"So there!" he called after her.

She ran up to her room and closed the door, in case Sukey should come and see her in tears. She had really burned her bridges behind her this time. Why had she been so savage with him? It was not on Sukey's account that she resented his ill manners, but on her own. He had chosen Lady Sara. He might as well have said it in so many words.

In the conservatory, Griffin carefully watered his plants, but his mind was elsewhere. It was ridiculous to call Sara vulgar. She was an accomplished lady—those marvelous Schubert songs ... If she was a little freer in her behavior than Sal, well, she was not a deb. She had made her debut before he left England. Sara must be five and twenty at least, but in an excellent state of preservation. And fond of travel. She had mentioned half a dozen times how she would have loved to see Brazil. That was the sort of lady to suit him. Not a missish, backward, clinging provincial like Myra. They were as different as day and night.

He heard a sound at the door and turned, thinking Sal had returned to apologize. He saw Sara, and was aware of a stab of disappointment.

"Am I intruding?" she asked, with a confident smile that assumed she was always welcome. She did not wait to be assured, but came in, looking around at his specimens. "So these are your specimens from South America. Tell me all about them, Griffin. I am appallingly ignorant, but eager to learn. What is this little one?"

"These are all bananas," he said, and told her a little about them.

"Let us have your gardener tend to this watering, Griffin. We have time for a stroll before dinner, just the two of us. The others have gone up to change."

"I don't allow my gardener to tend these specimens. Is it time to change for dinner?" he asked, drawing out his watch. "You're right. I had not realized it was so late. We must go."

"They won't start dinner without us," she laughed. "Do come into the rose garden. It is so romantic," she sighed. "The perfume fills the air at twilight, and the birds are singing." She looked at him archly, from the corner of her eyes. "And it is so very private," she said daringly.

Griffin knew it was his cue to kiss her. Strangely, he felt no overwhelming desire to do so. He liked to do his own courting. Sara had quite obviously come here to seduce him. He half admired her daring, but he was also a little shocked. Had things changed that much while he was away? Perhaps they had; he had been shocked by the waltz, too, but it was considered unexceptionable. He began to suspect that Alice was right. Beneath Sara's fine silk gown, there lurked the heart of a common hussy. Griffin did not consider this a deterrent. In fact, it excited him.

What he did object to was Sara's selfishness. She did not care if the rest of the table was kept waiting on her. She had enjoyed shocking the villagers in the drapery shop that morning. He had thought she was the antithesis of Myra—a mature, independent lady, but they had that selfishness and love of attention in common. Of course a lady reared to every sort of privilege would be selfish. How could she be otherwise? As to attention, he had no real aversion to it himself.

She smiled an invitation at him. He drew her into his arms and kissed her. Sara was no shrinking violet. She pressed herself against him quite wantonly, until he nearly forgot she was a lady. Then she drew back with a smile that was trying to look shy, but was, in fact, smug. "Shall we go to the garden now?" she said.

147

"I don't trust myself alone with you," he said. His voice was husky.

"Don't worry, I shan't let you get out of line, sir! I was not born yesterday."

"I have just had a scold for ignoring my guests. I think we had best not keep them waiting this time."

"Mothers can be such bores. But Lady Griffin is a darling. I quite dote on her."

Griffin did not correct her as to the deliverer of the scold. He went to the door and held it open. Lady Sara smiled on relentlessly. "Oh, by the by, Griffin, I have written a note to my Uncle Avery, who lives just ten miles beyond Headcorn. I thought we might take a spin over there in the morning, as we two are early birds. Avery is dying to hear of your travels. He will give us lunch, I expect."

"You forget, Mama is giving the guests a tour of the gardens tomorrow, Sara."

"But I have already had a tour, and you must be more than familiar with them."

"Actually I have not made a complete tour since returning. There have been many changes. I look forward to it."

"Ah, then I shall skip Uncle Avery's visit. Those gardens are worth careful study."

They mounted the stairs to their rooms together. Griffin wore a concentrated expression when he left her. She was a beautiful, desirable lady. But just a little encroaching, perhaps? He would assess her more carefully before coming to any conclusion.

Chapter Sixteen

Alice kept a close eye on Griffin that evening, and had to admit that he behaved with perfect propriety. As Lady Sara was a distinguished guest, she received a generous but not inordinate share of his attention. Naturally he had to stand up with her first, since she was the only titled lady present, barring his own mama. He did not have to look quite so happy about it, but it was a party after all, and he made a point to stand up with Sukey next. He stared pointedly at Alice as he approached Sukey, as if to say, I am being a good boy. She refused to smile at him, but she nodded her approval.

He danced with Miss Warwick from Headcorn, and, to judge by their smiles, gave several married ladies the thrill of the season by flirting delightfully with them. In fact, he danced with everyone he should except Alice herself. She felt the omission, but could not lay the offense in his dish, as she had as well as refused him in the conservatory.

Lady Sara got a little out of hand at the late supper. She sat at Griffin's right side, and did her best to monopolize his conversation. She could not feel a simple country party of sufficient import that the more formal rules of London need be obeyed—by her, at least. Griffin, aware of Alice's assessing stare, tried to divide his conversation with his other partner, but found it hard sledding. Sara kept harping at him.

"I hope you are going to play some waltzes, Griffin. What a dowdy party it will seem if you do not."

"I have held them off till after supper. I fear many of the local belles have not taken up the waltz yet. Not all the world is so dissipated as you and I," he joked.

This was exactly the sort of conversation to please her. Her eyes flashed a warm smile. "You and I are past redeeming, *ça va sans dire*. I had forgotten how outré these provincials are. How do they endure their assemblies, with no waltzing?"

"You are asking the wrong person, Sara. I endured five years without even the pleasure of a minuet, or country dance."

"Ah, but you had that famous tribal dance to take its place—to say nothing of Indian princesses. Not a word about a certain Princess Nwani. Travel is so broadening. I have been to the Continent, of course, but real travel to South America or Brazil—how I would love it."

"You might feel differently after taking a few meals from your lap, swatting midges and other insects."

"It would not bother me in the least. I like variety—midges and waltzes. We shall show the locals the way. Let us dance all the waltzes together."

"All of them?"

"Yes, why not? It is only a little country rout after all."

"But it is *my* part of the country, Sara. My reputation is already ragged after my recent set-to with Dunsmore."

"The man is a fool. Did I say *man*? That is an insult to *real* men like you."

Griffin did agree to have the first set of waltzes with Lady Sara. He had not much choice in the matter. Many of the provincial ladies had not yet learned the waltz. They were shuffling around the edge of the floor with their partners, but he sensed they would not like to expose their lack of skill to the local lord. Alice and Miss Sutton had moved in from the edges with their partners. Alice, he noticed, was standing up with Monty. He mentioned to Sara that he wondered what those two found to talk about.

"Why, they have been neighbors these five years. I should not be much surprised if there is a match hatching there."

"Monty and Alice Newbold?" he laughed. "Not a chance."

"Whyever not? You must have noticed how close they are. She ran over to sit by him the minute he arrived the first evening of our visit. The Newbolds are nothing special, of course. They have no noble connections whatsoever. If Myra had not nabbed Dunsmore, the younger sister would be doing well enough to marry Monty. I doubt her dot is as large as Myra's, and she lacks her sister's beauty. But I do not have to point out Myra's beauty to you, Griffin. You were the first to spot it," she said graciously. There was no danger from Myra; she could be an incomparable with no fear of competition.

Griffin was aware of a burning sensation deep in his chest. Monty and Alice? It was absurd. Yet it was Alice who had suggested he give Monty the dower house, and the job as his manager. She had spoken highly of him. Monty had been running tame in the neighborhood for five years. It was odd Sal had not accepted any of those offers she had been boasting of in London, now that he thought of it. He watched them as Monty whirled around the floor with Sara.

There was no lack of smiles and conversation. As he pondered the matter, Sara spoke. "I wonder if Miss Alice will have Montgomery, now that you are back. It was supposed that Monty would assume your title and estate. That was why he was permitted to dangle after her, I daresay. Now that you are back and have reclaimed Mersham, she may give him his congé."

"Alice is not like that," he said, a little hot under the collar. "If she loves him, she will marry him."

"Unless she can find herself a duke," Sara said sagely. "Sorry, Griffin, but you sounded so annoyed I could not resist needling you." The waltz ended.

Across the floor, Alice said, "You waltz very well, Monty."

"It is hot work, is it not?" he replied. "I believe I shall open the door for a breath of air."

"I shall go with you."

They strolled to the west door to catch the fragrance from the gardens. The moonlight lured them outside. It shone palely, turning the flowers into a ghost garden, etched in black and white. They remained on the doorstep, just looking and sniffing the perfume. The door swung to behind them, unnoticed.

"I have been meaning to thank you for putting in a good word for me, Miss Alice," Monty said. "Griffin mentioned the idea was yours."

"It was just common sense. Everyone knows you are an excellent manager."

"I was most surprised that the idea came from you. You did not care for me at first, I think?"

152

Alice's early animosity to Montgomery was only resentment of the idea that Griffin would not be returning. She had always regretted it, and this was the perfect time to apologize, as she did not wish to explain.

"I was only a child at the time. It was not that I did not care for you, Monty. Indeed, everyone speaks highly of you. Even Griffin thinks you have done a very good job."

"Kind of you to say so, my dear," he said, giving her shoulder an avuncular pat. "It did not help that I came to cuffs with Lady Griffin, and she removed to the dower house. I did not ask her to go, you know, though I own I did not try to prevent her."

The door opened abruptly, striking Alice a blow on the shoulder. Montgomery put out an arm to steady her. "Oh, it is you, Griffin," he said, surprised.

Griffin's sharp eyes glanced off the arm that was holding Alice. His expression stiffened. "Mama was wondering where you are, Alice," he lied. "Perhaps it would be best if Montgomery entertain you within doors. It looks a little fast, the two of you slipping out here."

"Just catching a breath of air," Montgomery explained. The aura of guilt that tinged his words had no cause except having offended his benefactor. "Shall we go in, Alice?" He left his hand on her arm to lead her inside.

Griffin just looked at the offending hand. It fell, and Montgomery said, "Or perhaps—er, I ought to run along and see if Lady Griffin would like a hand of cards."

"What an excellent idea," Griffin said, and held the door wide, closing it after him. Then he looked at Alice. "You must not follow Lady Sara's example and set up as a flirt, Alice. You are too green to handle the consequences."

"A flirt!" she exclaimed. "You mistake the matter, Griffin."

"Slipping away from a party with a gentleman might be construed that way."

"That did not bother you when I slipped away from Lady Calmet's ball with you."

"That was different."

"Yes, the difference being that Mr. Montgomery is always well behaved, whereas Lord Griffin carries a certain aroma of the jungle."

"Don't try to distract me. It is not my behavior that is at question here, miss."

"Nor have you any right to question mine, or Monty's for that matter. He would never do what you are suggesting."

"Then what propelled the two of you out here, into the moonlight." He glanced up at the gibbous moon.

"The heat, Griffin. We are not so inured to tropical climes as you."

"And that is all?"

"What do you mean?" she demanded.

"Such a romantic setting, it seems a likely spot for a proposal. Are you and Monty thinking of making a match?"

Her blank expression was answer enough. "Where on earth did you get such an idea?"

"Well, you were standing up with him."

"I have stood up with half a dozen gentlemen I am more likely to marry than Montgomery." Griffin looked toward the garden. He was beginning to feel a little foolish. "You must be mad," she said. "Monty is thirty-five if he is a day. He is practically old enough to be my father. Is that why you came out here, because you actually thought he was trying to set up a flirtation with me?"

"Of course not," he said brusquely. "I just wanted a breath of air myself, and razzed Monty from habit. Lovely night, is it not?"

"It was," she said stiffly, and opened the door. Griffin followed her back into the ballroom, trying to put a decent face on his latest piece of folly.

The music began. "I am an idiot," he said. "Dance with me, Sal, to show me you don't hate me."

"I could not be bothered to hate you," she said.

Griffin swept her into his arms, wondering how he had come to get so upset over nothing. What difference did it make if Sal did marry Monty? The man was not a monster after all. A dull old stick, of course, but hardly like to beat his wife, or put her in the poor house.

They danced half the waltz without speaking. To break the stretching silence, Griffin said, "Cat got your tongue, Sal? You are quiet, all of a sudden."

Alice decided Griffin had only been doing his duty, if his mama had indeed been worried at her absence. "Just sulking," she said, "but I am over it now. I must congratulate you on your improved manners, Griffin. I believe you have stood up with all the young ladies this evening. Lady Sara cannot be so bossy as I thought either, or she would not have permitted it."

"I have heeded your reprimand that a gentleman cannot be led against his wishes. Not by bossy commands, at any rate. We are more easily led by guile."

"Yet it was my bossy command that spurred your reformation," she pointed out, with a pert grin.

"Logic was never my strong suit," he admitted. "I am a creature of intuition."

"Sukey would like to see the voodoo doll, and the knives and things," Alice said a moment later.

"Has she snipped off a piece of my hair, to attach to it? I am referring to my outrageous treatment of her and her mama during this visit."

"No, not *yours*. You have weaseled your way back into her approval by standing up with her, and by showing her the prince's letter."

"She forgives easily. If not mine, then whose?"

"That would be indiscreet of me to say, but if Lady S***, as they say in the journals, believes in this black magic, she had best burn those torn stockings, or they will be taken from her dustbin. Actually, Miss Warwick would like to see the things, too. Would it be possible to have a few friends out tomorrow afternoon?"

"Invite anyone you like. I shall make myself available for a lecture, if it would please you."

"Lady Sara does not have other plans?" she asked, surprised at his new acquiescence.

"I don't know what Lady Sara's plans may be, but I shall be here, to entertain all my guests."

He was soon busy entertaining some of those guests on the dance floor. Miss Warwick was surprised to be asked to stand up for the next waltz. She waltzed very badly, but Griffin was so nice about her stepping on his toes that she fell in love with him on the spot.

As so few of the others waltzed, a country-dance was called. The rout was considered a great success. When the party broke up, Lady Sara suggested a cup of cocoa before retiring, for those who were houseguests.

"We have earned it," she said, with a weary sigh. "So fatiguing, entertaining the provincial neighbors, but it must be done occasionally. One never knows when their support will be needed for elections, and things."

"Quite," Griffin smiled blandly, but he was beginning to understand how Lady Sara's mind worked.

"I thought it was a lovely party," Mrs. Sutton said, and received support from her daughter and Alice.

Sensing that she was being sent to Coventry, Lady Sara was the picture of agreeableness the next morning during the garden tour. She knew more about flowers than the rest of the guests put together, and could praise more effectively. She attended the lecture on the Brazilian trophies in the afternoon, although she had heard the same thing in London, and poured tea when the lecture was over.

A few friends were invited to dinner that evening. After dinner, Lady Griffin said, "Perhaps Lady Sara will play for us, if we ask her very nicely."

"Or even if we don't," Mrs. Sutton murmured under her breath to Sukey.

Griffin overheard it, and chewed a smile. Sara allowed herself to be cajoled into entertaining them with a piano recital, and the party removed to the music room. Alice arrived late, and sat in the back row, near the door. As the rousing strains of *Rastlose Liebe* rent the air, she found her head began to pound. Perhaps they would be spared *Meerestille* and *Erlkönig*. But when the first bout of clapping died away, Lady Sara smiled and said, "*Meerestille*." There was to be no reprieve. As the white hands arched over the keyboard, Alice decided to slip away and return when the recital was over.

She wandered first to the saloon, then off to the library. The latter was in darkness, but at the end of the corridor, she noticed a light coming from the conservatory, and decided to go there. Griffin's gardener must be tending the plants. She would have him show her the orchids, as he used to do when she was a child.

She opened the door and slipped in. There, at his usual bench, sat Griffin with his head bent over a text. He looked up with a guilty start. "Sal, what are you doing here?"

"I have a headache from—that is—what are you doing here? I thought you were in the music room. Do you not know Lady Sara is performing her Schubert pieces?"

"Yes, I was standing at the back. Lovely music, but I just slipped out for a moment to check on some of my seedlings. They seem to be wilting. I think they are getting too much sun. They grow under the shelter of the forest in the Amazon. I have put them under the palms."

"Oh, then you will want to return to the music room. Don't feel you must accompany me."

"There is no hurry. Sara's selections last for half an hour." He had thoroughly enjoyed the performance the other night, and could not account for the air of ennui that had seized him when she struck up the same pieces tonight. The air of novelty was lacking, perhaps. Or perhaps his chief delight had been in the performer. He was rapidly losing interest in Sara Winsley.

"Then you will catch the last piece if you go now." Still he seemed reluctant to leave. "Are you afraid I shall kill your plants with my brown thumb? Don't worry. I shan't disturb them."

"I am not afraid of that. You never were an obstreperous child, like some visitors. No, I was just relaxing. I feel most at home here, surrounded by my plants. A nightingale has got into the conservatory. It was singing, just now, in the palm trees. Is that not enchanting?"

"Oh, I should love to hear it."

"Listen," he said. They stood still, staring into the dense foliage. After a moment, the sweet sound of the nightingale floated on the air.

A radiant smile beamed on Alice's face as she listened. "It almost seems like magic, as if the plants were singing. It won't harm the plants, will it?" she asked.

"I shouldn't think so. Birds and plants go together, like love and marriage."

"It is odd, is it not, how such an insignificant-looking bird has such a beautiful song. She sings like an angel."

"He!"

"You cannot possibly know that!"

"Of course I can. That is the male's mating call. You must allow that I am familiar with *that* role. And like this poor nightingale, cut off from the females, I sing in vain."

"You should let the bird go."

"I would prefer to open the door, and let in a mate. It would be nice to have a pair of birds in the conservatory."

"But the nightingale is not very pretty."

"Birds are like books; you don't judge them by their covering. There are magnificent birds in Brazil. Macaws, parrots, . . . All colors of the rainbow. And the butterflies, as big as birds and so colorful. I wanted to bring some birds home, but could not deprive them of their freedom."

"You brought Snow White home."

"A fellow sold her to me on board the ship. I only took her because he kept her locked in a miserable little cage in the hold. The poor thing was close to expiring."

He indicated a seat by the desk, and sat down beside Alice. "I have come to a decision, Sal," he said pensively.

Her heart tightened to a ball in her chest. "Lady Sara?" she asked, with admirable calmness.

"No, not Lady Sara. Not anyone. I have decided I shall not get married right away at all. It is foolish to pitch myself into a hasty marriage only because Myra jilted me. That would be mere pride. You said I should not let a lady bearlead me, and it is Myra leading me to think I must marry soon, to show the world my heart is not broken. Well, it is not broken, but it is cracked a little. A man cannot really fall in love until his heart is whole. I shall let my heart heal itself, then I shall find a bride."

A sense of peace fell over Alice at his words. Not Lady Sara! "What about Greece?" she asked.

"Next year, or the next year after that. That was mere running away, too. I have tons of categorizing and writing to do before I leave. I shall send the guests home at the appointed time, and get down to some serious work. You will be joining your family in London, I think?"

"Yes, for Myra's wedding."

"I want to give the couple something, but am uncertain what would be acceptable. I thought I might call the white orchid the Dunsmore Orchid, in honor of the couple, and in an effort to patch up old scars. What do you think?"

"They will like that," she said simply, but she knew Myra would like it better if it were called for her alone.

The nightingale sang again, and during its song they were silent. Griffin looked at Alice and smiled a gentle, sad smile.

"You seem happier, yet sadder somehow, Griffin," she said.

"I think it is called growing up, Sal. I blame this ill-mannered whelp you have been seeing on the death throes of a youthful dream. I was going to come home, marry Myra, and become a famous botanist. But botanists are not famous. What people want are circuses: black magic and tales of native barbarism. They don't really care about science, and there is no reason why the world should share my particular interest. I was as childish as Myra. Of what use is fame? It is the work that matters. And, of course, love. I have my work. One day, I shall find the other necessity."

"That sounds very sensible."

"And very unlike Griffin," he added with a smile. "You have been extraordinarily patient with me. I want to thank you—for that, and for showing me the folly of my ways. What a wise little thing you are. We had best go back to the music room. How is the headache?"

"It is still nagging a little. I shall go to bed. Will you make my apologies to your mama?"

"Of course."

They walked together down the hall to the staircase. After they said good night, Griffin watched a moment as Alice ascended the stairs, then he returned to the music room.

In her room, Alice's first sense of relief was rapidly dwindling, leaving a void behind. She was glad she had saved Griffin from Myra, and from Lady Sara. She honestly felt that neither lady was right for him, but the final victory still evaded her. He did not love her. All she had done was set him free to fall in love with someone else.

Chapter Seventeen

The next two days were enjoyable, but Alice could not honestly say she made a single inch of headway with Griffin. He took each of the young ladies out for a drive in his dashing new curricle and team of grays, and let Alice and Lady Sara try the reins. Sukey declined. In various groups, the guests toured the house and gardens, visited neighbors, and went to a fair. It was during a call at Warwick's that the idea of going to the fair in Ashford came up, and Griffin invited Nancy to go with them. Alice took it as a compliment to herself as Nancy was her friend, but other than that, Griffin did not distinguish her from the other guests. He was pleasant and considerate, but he kept some vital part of himself locked away.

The morning rides now included Sukey and Alice, as well as Griffin and Lady Sara. Lady Sara distinguished herself by riding faster and jumping her mount higher than the other ladies, but she failed to impress her target. The harder she tried, the farther Griffin seemed to slip away from her.

When she received a note from her Uncle Avery inviting her to take part in the local hunt, she cut her visit short by one day and left. Avery had informed her that Lord Sethmore, an eligible parti, was staying with him.

The last day of the visit, without Lady Sara, was the most enjoyable of all. Everyone, including Lady Griffin and Mrs. Sutton, drove to Tunbridge Wells. The elder ladies took the waters in the pump room, while the others roamed the town, poking through the shops, strutting on the pantiles, and generally behaving like tourists. They ate at an inn and returned in time for dinner.

"We ought to have invited your friend, Miss Warwick," Griffin said to Alice when they returned.

Alice sensed a growing warmth between these two, and as Nancy would be staying behind after she left, Alice was a little bothered by it.

"She will be coming this evening," she reminded him.

For that last evening, a party of youngsters had been invited in for dinner. Mrs. Sutton played the piano afterward, and they had a few country-dances. Alice kept a sharp eye on Nancy Warwick and Griffin, but could discern no dangerous intimacy between them.

It had been settled that the Suttons would return to London in the morning, taking Alice with them. At the last minute, Alice received a letter from her mama, asking her to bring a few items from Newbold Hall that had been forgotten in their hasty departure.

"I am sorry to delay you, Mrs. Sutton. I shall ride over to Newbold. It won't take me a minute," Alice said.

"Send a footman," Lady Griffin suggested.

"The servants would not know what Mama

163

wants. She especially asks for a list she has been working on for weeks. It contains last minute details regarding the wedding. I know the one she means, but there are half a dozen places it might be, and it would be a tragedy if the wrong list were sent. She has dozens of lists all over the house."

"You will have to change into your habit. I daresay it has already been packed," Mrs. Sutton pointed out.

"Oh, dear! I am sorry to detain you."

"I'll take you in my new curricle," Griffin said.

"The very thing. Thank you, Griffin."

She got her bonnet and pelisse, and they left while the others were still at breakfast. Leaden skies threatened an unpleasant trip to London, but the rain did not come yet. Nothing of much interest was said during this last interval when Alice was alone with Griffin. They congratulated themselves on how well the weather had held up for the visit. Alice thanked him for the party; they discussed when the Newbolds might return to Newbold Hall, and Griffin mentioned some articles he was writing for the scientific journals. The name Miss Warwick did not arise.

He waited in the saloon while Alice and the servants dashed about, collecting the items on Mrs. Newbold's list. The wedding list in particular proved troublesome, but was finally discovered stuck in a recent copy of *La Belle Assemblée*, marking the page that showed the wedding gown Myra had chosen. Alice grabbed it and returned to the saloon.

"All set!" she said, waving the list.

She took her leave of the servants, and they returned to the curricle. As they drove toward Mersham, Griffin said, "There is something I want to ask your opinion about, Sal."

Her heart did not speed. "Ask your opinion" had not the possibilities of "something I want to ask you."

"What is it?"

"Mama and I have received invitations to Myra's wedding. As it is in London, Mama does not plan to attend. They won't expect her to. She seldom goes to London. Do you think I ought to accept? If the invitation was sent as a peace offering, I would feel loutish to refuse. London is not far enough away to serve as an excuse for an able-bodied young man. If it is a mere courtesy, then I daresay they are hoping I don't show up. Did Myra discuss it with you?"

"No. After all the fracas, I just assumed you would not be invited. But, of course, we have been good neighbors forever, and I am glad they asked you, even if you choose not to attend." She waited to hear his verdict. "Will you go?" she asked a moment later.

"I could use the excuse of a pressing engagement elsewhere. Perhaps that would excuse me, without trodding on anyone's sensitivities."

"Yes," she said, her voice small with disappointment.

"You think I should go," he said.

"I truly don't know what Mama had in mind when she invited you."

His head turned, and he smiled. "I have it! Ask Myra what she had in mind when you see her, and drop me a line as soon as you learn. You don't mind?"

"No, not at all."

"I knew you would not object to the bother—you have done me greater favors in the past. What I meant was whether you objected to writing to a bachelor."

"Don't be silly, Griffin. I agreed to write to you

165

from London before, if Dunsmore appeared to be getting the inside track."

"I noticed you did not write, though."

"He did not have the inner track at that time. I don't think of you as a bachelor."

"There is a facer for me," he laughed. "I am beneath consideration as a *parti*, eh?"

"You know perfectly well it is not that. It is just that we have been friends from the egg. I shall be writing your mama a bread-and-butter letter, and shall enclose a note for you. What could be more proper than that? The postman—and the villagers—will never know how I am pursuing you."

He smiled pensively. "You never did pursue, Sal. Perhaps that is why you are so comfortable to be with."

Alice felt like a traitor, holding her guilty secret to her breast. She sensed that he was referring not only to Lady Sara, but to the hordes of females who chased him in London, and was glad that he did not include her among them.

The Suttons were ready to leave when they reached Mersham. There was a spate of giving thanks and leave-taking. Griffin accompanied them to the carriage. They drew away just as the first fat drops fell with a plop on the roof. Alice watched with a sad twisting of her heart as Griffin scuttled into the house. Was this what he meant by *saudades*? He waved from the doorway. Alice waved back.

"What a lovely visit," Sukey said.

The trip passed quickly despite the rain. Mrs. Sutton was as good a gossip as the girls, and they all three crowed over Lady Sara's defeat.

"If I had to listen to those three German tunes one more time, I would have plugged my ears,"

Mrs. Sutton declared. "Griffin is fortunate to have avoided that fate. Imagine having to listen to her barrage of culture for the rest of your life. I hear she is off after Sethmore."

The carriage pulled up at Berkeley Square in mid-afternoon. As soon as the greetings were over and the items just retrieved from Newbold were turned over, Alice inquired about Griffin's wedding invitation.

"Do you really want him to come, Mama, or was it a courtesy invitation?" she asked.

"I could hardly not send his mama a card when we have been neighbors for twenty-five years. How could I invite her and not Griffin? He will have the sense to refuse. Myra does not want him here, to destroy her special day."

Alice looked for Myra's opinion, as it was really her feelings Griffin was interested in.

Myra looked hatefully smug. She glanced at Dunsmore, who sat with the ladies. "What do you think, Dunny?"

"What is the point discussing it? He has the invitation. He will come if he wants to, stirring up trouble. No way of preventing it." He began rubbing his arm, which troubled him at the very name of Griffin.

"He won't stir up trouble," Alice said. "He is quite resigned to the match." Myra just looked at her, as if she were a bedlamite.

"If he behaves himself, there is no harm in his coming, I suppose," Dunsmore conceded gracelessly.

Short of announcing that she was going to write to Griffin, Alice could not push the issue any further. It was pretty clear that her mama and Dunsmore wanted Griffin to stay away. Myra, she thought, would enjoy another display of Griffin's undying devotion.

167

Alice went upstairs and wrote her letters, a thank-you note to Lady Griffin, with an enclosure to Griffin. "You are off the hook," she wrote bluntly. "Mama does not expect you to come; Dunsmore's arm hurt him at the very idea, and Myra only wants to flaunt your broken heart." This sounded so curt when she read it over that she added a post-script. "But if you want to come, please do. I would like to see you."

Then she hastily sealed up the letters, and took them belowstairs to place on the mail salver for posting. The modiste was coming to put the finishing touches on the wedding gowns that afternoon, so there was no outing.

That evening they were invited to dinner with Dunsmore's relatives, a dull scald but considered a great step up socially. The party consisted largely of Cabinet ministers, the conversation of the Corn Laws. It seemed the height of irony that Lady Sara was there, and played her three tunes for the guests after dinner. Alice could only assume she had managed to lose Sethmore with even greater haste than she had lost Griffin. It would be a kind-ness if someone would tell her not to try so hard. Any animal will run when it is chased.

The wedding drew nearer, with frenzy growing at each passing day. The Season was officially over, but those debs who had made a match and wanted to have their wedding at St. George's in Hanover Square lingered on, throwing little intimate parties of thirty or forty people. Myra and Dunsmore were invited to most of them, and of course the invita-tions included Alice and her mama. The theaters were still open as well, so that there was no short-age of entertainment.

Griffin's polite refusal to the wedding arrived,

bearing the excuse of a heavy load of work after his trip.

"Poor Griffin," Myra said, sighing over the note. "He decided he could not bear the sight of me marrying Dunny after all. It is very sad, really. I shouldn't be surprised to see him lurking in the back row at the church. You know how people cannot help prodding an old pain."

"Yes, I know what you mean," Alice replied, with an unusual degree of feeling.

The ache in her heart did not go away, nor even diminish. She kept thinking of Griffin, wondering what he was doing, and with whom. He had been quite attentive to Nancy Warwick. Perhaps, in his loneliness, he was seeking comfort there. She was sorry she had told him not to come for the wedding. It would have been a chance to see him again. She had a feeling she would not see much of him after she returned home. That little constraint due to his ruptured engagement would keep him away, and his work would keep him busy.

Chapter Eighteen

"You are off the hook. Mama does not expect you to come." Griffin read it with a sense of relief. To see Myra again would be like returning to the scene of an unpleasant experience—a death, perhaps, or the drawing of a bad tooth. That period of his life was over, and he was happy in his work. Colleagues came to Mersham to lighten the loneliness of long evenings. These colleagues were invariably males, however, and Griffin soon realized something vital was missing in his existence. An emptiness would settle on him at odd hours, a sense, almost, of futility.

That familiar sensation was particularly strong on the eve of Myra's wedding, as he worked in his conservatory. Marriage had been on his mind a good deal that day. Time lent a charm to his old error. He missed his romantic memories of Myra, but he did not miss her, or want her. He wanted a woman, of course, but not just a woman. It was the fulfillment of marriage and children that he craved. His wife would have to be a special sort of lady, someone who would not object to his occasional trips, or preferably agree to accompany him. If she could take an interest in his work, that would be ideal, but at least she must be able to amuse herself in some sensible manner while he worked. Such ladies, he feared, were few and far between. Myra would have been a disaster. Lady Sara was a better match, but pretty as she was, he had not warmed to her. She had been on the town too long, was too fast, too experienced, too predatory. A younger lady would suit him better.

The nightingale suddenly burst into song, as it often did. It never failed to enchant him. Its futile warbling for a mate reminded him of himself. He had left the conservatory door open several times, but the bird never left, and no mate came to him. He listened, remembering the evening it had first sung for him. Alice had been here . . .

He often thought of Alice. Her having grown up was a vivid reminder that he was getting on himself. She had been in pigtails when he left, and was a young lady when he returned. A very pretty young lady. He was aware of the growing attachment to her. But Myra's sister. God, what a fool he would look, running from one Newbold girl to the other. People would think he was trying to hold on to some part of Myra. Not that the girls were anything alike. They could hardly be more different. Now that the scales had fallen from his eyes, he judged Myra more rationally. A spoiled, inane beauty, who thought of nothing but herself.

Sal had hit it on the head. Myra only wanted him to come to her wedding to flaunt his broken heart. He was through with being led by what Myra wanted. He would stay away to spite her. He felt a sense of frustration, and eventually figured out that what was bothering him was that he *wanted* to attend that wedding—not to see Myra, but to see Alice. And he was staying away because of Myra, still being led by her.

He remembered Alice laughing with him and at him, scolding him and advising, coming to his conservatory and asking him questions about Brazil. She knew a lot about Brazil, more than most people. She must have been reading up on it. Odd that she should. Unless . . .

But that was ridiculous. Alice didn't love him. She was only a— But she wasn't a child any longer. She was a lady now. The nightingale called again, and he was ambushed by a sudden memory of Alice's radiant face when she had first heard it. It was the same expression she had worn when they first met in Calmet's saloon in London, after his trip. A look of enchantment, almost of love. How had he been so blind?

He wanted to rush to his curricle that instant and head for London. Of course he would go to the wedding—but he had sent in his refusal. No matter, he could crouch in the back row. Alice would see him. He hadn't a doubt in the world that she would feel his presence. He would find a moment alone with her somehow, and test her feelings. Was he imagining that she cared for him? He felt no doubt at all of his feelings for her. This love had been growing insensibly ever since his return, perhaps ever since his departure for Brazil. He remembered she had stood at the roadside, waving and smiling heroically through her tears. He had looked in vain for Myra; she had been too distraught to leave her room.

He strode into the house, to find his mama sitting with Monty, making him play cards with her. How she abused the poor soul. After threatening to not let him step a toe into Mersham, she ended up sending for him two nights out of three.

"I have decided to take a run up to London, Mama," he said.

"When, tomorrow?"

"No, tonight."

"Why, James? This is very sudden, is it not?"

"Yes, I just decided."

"But you won't arrive till the middle of the night. Why do you not wait till morning?"

"I want to be there in the morning. Myra is being married at eleven."

"You sent in a refusal! You cannot go scrambling in without an invitation. I thought you had got over that miserable girl. Don't go making a cake of yourself. If you are going to stand up and shout when the minister asks if there is any reason why this couple should not be married, I shall go with you," she said, pulling herself up from her chair. "I always wanted to see that."

"By Jove," Monty said. "Not the thing, Griffin."

"Don't be an ass, Monty. I am not going to make trouble."

"Then why go at all?" his mama repeated.

"Because I want to see a wedding. I have not seen one for over five years." He ran, laughing, upstairs.

Lady Griffin looked at Monty. "He was quite ill in the jungle, you must know. I daresay whatever rot got at him took a nibble from the brain. That is my trick, I believe," she said, and picked up the cards.

Griffin had his valet pack his formal suit and a few changes of linen. He was unsure how long the Newbolds meant to remain in London, but he doubted they would dart back to Newbold the next day. Within half an hour, he was seated in his carriage, being driven through the night to London. A strange euphoria had descended on him. It was as if a great load had been removed from his chest. He was in love with Alice. Beautiful little brat, Sal Newbold.

He went to bed at six o'clock in the morning, and slept till ten. He did not plan to notify Sal of his arrival. He would surprise her. At ten he arose, made a careful toilette, and called for his carriage.

"St. George's, Hanover Square," he directed his groom.

On Berkeley Square, the day began long before ten. Mrs. Newbold was up at seven. Myra, who had not slept a wink all night, was up at eight, and Alice joined them at eight-thirty, already wearing her wedding outfit. Myra had not wanted Sal to wear white. She wore a pale mint green gown, her favorite color, trimmed with small pink roses around the bodice. Her hair was dressed *en corbeille*, with a band of rosebuds in lieu of a hat. She was happy with the outfit and her looks, and only wished that Griffin could see her looking so stylish. The day had lost its euphoria for her when she learned that Griffin would not be there.

The house was in chaos, with the coiffeur arranging Myra's hair, while Myra watched, holding a mirror in front of her, and complaining at every stroke of the brush. Alice was sent scampering off checking for gloves and shawls, and to make sure the guests who were putting up with the Newbolds were comfortable. Forgotten items had to be packed in Myra's trunks. A few gifts arrived, and were taken for the bride's approval.

"Another set of silver candlesticks. Good God, where will we put them? Thank goodness Dunny has four houses. We will need them to hold all this rubbish."

"They are sterling silver, my dear," her mama pointed out apologetically. She felt that Myra was already a duchess. She could hardly wait to add "Your Grace" to her apologies.

"How is the back of my hair, Mama? It looks horrid in front. Dunny won't have me when he sees how ugly I look."

"You look like an angel, dear. Don't fret. Alice, fetch Myra a cup of tea. She is looking peckish."

"If I ever get married, I shall elope," Alice said firmly, and went to order the tea.

It was finally time to set out for Hanover Square. The Newbolds went in their family carriage, but it was inside the duke's strawberry-bedecked doors that the new duchess would drive to the Pulteny for her wedding breakfast. Mrs. Newbold had not felt up to entertaining her noble in-laws at Berkeley Square.

Lord Griffin was already seated in the last row when the wedding party entered the Corinthian portico of St. George's. Alice was too excited to feel his presence. The ceremony proceeded with no disruptions, except a slight delay when Dunsmore dropped the ring. Alice retrieved it, and watched with a sense of awe as the couple made their fateful vows. "To have and to hold, from this day forward." What a huge undertaking marriage was. Imagine Myra promising to love the duke for the rest of her life, or even for a day.

Yet it looked like love shining in Myra's eyes when the duke slid the ring on her finger. Perhaps it was just delight at being a duchess. She was a duchess now, Alice supposed. Whoever Griffin married would be a countess. Lady Griffin. Surely he would not make Nancy Warwick a countess! She was on thorns to return to Newbold Hall, and learn what was happening during her absence.

The ceremony was over, and Myra took her first walk as the Duchess of Dunsmore, down the aisle on her duke's trembling arm. Alice fell into place behind. She found herself searching the pews for friends. She spotted Sukey Sutton and her mama amid the throng who were not actually invited, but had come to see the show. Sukey surreptitiously lifted her hand and moved her fingers in a wave. Alice smiled but was prevented by the solemnity of the occasion from returning the wave. Her eyes moved over the rows, back toward the rear of the church. She could stare as much as she wanted, because everyone was looking at the bride. Everyone except one man in the back row, who looked straight ahead.

She looked, and looked again. It couldn't be. But it was; it was Griffin. He had come after all, just as Myra said he would. It was he, lurking in the back row, prodding his pain. She lowered her brows in a dark scowl when she caught his eye. He smiled, trying to conceal his pain. The wedding couple continued on out the door.

There was a general melee of friends congratulating the couple, and soon of the carriages arriving. Alice looked all around for Griffin, and saw him hanging at the edge of the crowd, waiting. She marched straight to him.

"I told you not to come," she said. "You look like the ghost at the feast. It is too late, Griffin. She is married. I thought you would have more pride than to come."

"I want to talk to you, Sal."

"You obviously cannot talk to me here, and now. We are leaving for the Pulteny. Some of the guests are coming to Berkeley Square after to dance. Myra

176

and the duke will not stay long. If you want to call in the evening, around seven, I shall sneak into the library for a talk."

"I don't intend to sneak around. I was invited to this do. I doubt your mama will throw me out if I appear for the dance."

"It is too late, Griffin. Take your last look now. See, she is just waving from Dunsmore's carriage."

The duchess spotted Griffin. She smiled an exultant smile, pointed him out to her duke, and waved her final adieu. Griffin blew her a kiss. The duchess was hard-pressed to explain his merry smile, but she was pleased with the kiss.

"Save me a dance, Sal," Griffin said, then he turned and strode down the street, swinging his cane and whistling.

Chapter Nineteen

Such a Lucullan feast as graced the table of the Pulteny Hotel had not been seen since the Prince Regent entertained Czar Alexander and King Frederick of Prussia and their noble minions. There were more courses and removes, more wines and sweets and savories than Alice had ever seen collected in one place before. Quails and hares and beef fillets larded with anchovies were removed by truffled pullets and hens in aspic. They all tasted like wood to Alice. Even the grand finale of a subtlety fashioned in sugar to resemble Dunsmore's ancestral castle failed to amuse.

Alice had a perfectly miserable dinner. She was filled with sadness to think that Myra was leaving her home forever. Before Dunsmore's entrance into their lives, she and Myra had been friends, and she missed that earlier camaraderie. The greater exacerbation, however, was to know that Griffin had not gotten over Myra. It infuriated her that he had come creeping to the wedding for a last look at her.

She was sorry for his pain, but she would not indulge it.

She would tell him quite frankly that he must pull himself together, and if he could not, then he was not fit for civilization. He must return to the jungle and learn to live in a tree. Her mama, mistaking her mood for jealousy, tried to console her.

"Don't mope, Alice. You shall do as well next year," she said. "We move in ducal circles now. You will spend the Season with the duchess. Myra will find a parti for you. The Marquess of Lansdowne is on the lookout for a bride, you must know."

"And has been for the past decade," Alice muttered. The chinless marquess chose that moment to drool a smile at her.

Alice felt very much like crying, but she smiled dutifully, and drank some wine, for the food refused to go down her throat. Eventually the dinner and speeches and toasts were over, and they could go home to begin the dancing. She was angry that Griffin was coming, and half-afraid that he would not. In any case, she meant to detour him from the ballroom to a private parlor for his scold.

The duke and duchess opened the dancing. They gazed soulfully into each other's eyes, and exchanged not a word. Everyone agreed they made a handsome couple. Myra could not like to leave such a stunning party too early, and hung on until the shadows of evening lengthened. The duke was eager to be on his way; he disliked to travel after dark. All the while they danced, Alice was on nettles lest Griffin come pouncing in and cause a scene.

It was eight o'clock before the bridal couple was finally bounced off amid a shower of blessing and teasing. Alice breathed a sigh of relief. At least Griffin had missed them. At nine, she began to wonder what kept him. By nine-thirty, she was wishing he would come. There could be no harm in it now. Instead of a scolding, she would try to cheer him up. At ten the last carriage left, leaving behind the guests who were to spend the night and return later to Newbold Hall with Mrs. Newbold.

This family party was wending its way back to the ballroom after seeing the guests off when the door knocker sounded. Alice hung behind. She had given up on Griffin's coming, thinking he had either drunk himself into a stupor or had taken her advice and stayed away. But still she dallied, just in case.

"Is Miss Alice in?" a man's voice inquired. She recognized it at once, and flew to the door, her heart hammering.

Griffin! He sounded completely sober, thank God. He had changed into evening clothes, and looked so dashing she could only wonder at Myra's choosing the duke. His bronzed skin was accentuated by the white cravat at his throat. At his ear, the gold earring twinkled. She was glad he had waited this late, or Myra might have changed her mind, even if she was already married. How his eyes sparkled. "Myra has already left," she said.

He followed her into the saloon, where a riot of glasses and shawls and confusion reigned after the recent revels.

"I know. I waited outside until the last carriage had left. You were right. It would have been gauche of me to come and dance at Myra's wedding. How did it go off?"

"Fine. Very well," she said, scouring her mind for something of interest to add. "Dunsmore dropped the ring."

"Butterfingers."

She sensed a lack of ease in him, a nervousness,

as he paced to and fro, glancing around at the aftermath of the party. His nervousness transferred itself to Alice. Her various speeches flew from her mind, leaving her at a loss for words. He did not look morose, as she expected, nor vindictive, as she feared, but there was some tension in him. It hit her like a bolt of lightning. He is leaving! He has come to make his farewells before going to Greece, or some other impossible place. He cannot endure England without Myra, and he is going to run away.

"What was it you wanted to see me about?" Her voice came out shrill and louder than she intended. She meant to be calm, polite. She had endured the rest of it; she could take this final blow, too, like a lady.

Griffin tossed his shoulders. "I don't know how to begin." He was half a room away, and he did not come closer. The glow in his eyes was strong, but unreadable. "I have been such a fool."

Alice decided he had come for comfort, and adjusted her mood accordingly. She found a wine decanter and glasses, and poured two glasses. When she sat on the satin-striped sofa, Griffin joined her.

"A toast?" she suggested. "To Myra and the duke."

"Let us make that, 'the duke and duchess.' I think she would prefer it that way."

They exchanged a small smile of mutual understanding and drank. "I am sorry it did not work out for you, Griffin," she said. "I hope you will not think too badly of her. It was not just the superior title, you know. She truly does like that sort of man—easy to get on with, quiet."

"Biddable. She chose well to refuse me. I would have led her a hellish life. Hellish for *her*, I mean," he added hastily, not wanting to cut the ground

181

from under his feet. "I trust some ladies would not object too strenuously to my nature, and my work."

Alice listened, trying to hear what was being communicated beneath the words. Was he going to discuss other ladies with her? She really did not feel she could endure that tonight, after her wretched day.

"Very likely," she said dampingly. "Lady Sara, perhaps," she added, as the silence stretched uncomfortably between them.

"No, I prefer a younger, less sophisticated lady. Perhaps my long sojourn in the jungle has left me in arrears of the fashion, but I feel more comfortable with a simpler lady. I do not mean simple of mind, of course, but less versed in the ways of the fashionable world."

Immediately the name Miss Warwick popped into Alice's head. He was apologizing for her provincial manner. She felt her heart sink. He had convinced himself he was in love with Nancy Warwick, to assuage his grief at losing Myra. "It might be wiser for you to put some time between your recent loss and choosing a new wife, if that is what you are talking about," she said, observing him closely. "You mentioned the need of a whole heart, you recall." She read his quick frown, and feared he had already offered for Nancy. Impetuous fool!

"Do me the courtesy of allowing that I know my own mind—and heart," he said gruffly.

"That is news to me, Griffin. You loved Myra until a few weeks ago. You were mooning all over Lady Sara at your house party, now you have suddenly found some provincial miss. I give it a month."

"You sound as though I were an acknowledged here and therein," he objected. "I had never been in love when I proposed to Myra. To tell the truth,

I hardly knew her. She was beautiful and shy and admired me. I have been in love with a dream for five years, not a lady."

"Are you sure this is not a dream, too, Griffin? You expect this simple miss to be at home in the wilds of the world?"

"Italy and Greece are hardly the wilds of the world."

"If your mind is made up, I don't know why you bother talking to me about it," she said with an angry toss of her shoulders.

"Who else should I speak to?" he said, confused at her lack of sympathy. "Who else but you ever understood me, Sal? At least I thought you understood me." He peered for her reaction. Had he imagined she was fond of him?

"No, I never understood you at all," she said baldly. "I thought you were beginning to have some sense, but I see you are as incomprehensible as ever."

"Then you don't think it would work?"

"I have no idea. Why ask me? Ask Miss Warwick—if you have not done so already."

Griffin blinked in bewilderment. "Miss—who?"

"Miss Warwick. Is that not the provincial miss you have in mind?"

"I don't know what you are—oh, the girl from the village who wanted to see my trophies. Your friend that we took to the fair at Ashmore."

Alice gazed at him, while a wild idea sprouted at the back of her mind. He didn't even remember Nancy's name. He had been at Mersham; there were no other eligible ladies nearby. Griffin watched as hope grew to knowledge, and gradually trembled to joy.

He pulled her into his arms, laughing in relief, and cradled her against his chest. "You scared the life out of me, Sal. I have been a fool. It was you all the time, and I was too blind to see it."

She peered up from his shoulder, tears misting her eyes. It was like a dream finally come true. "But you hardly know me, Griffin."

"I have known you from the cradle."

"Since I am grown up, I mean."

A tender smile settled on his harsh features. Some trace of the twelve-year-old lingered in her youthful smile, and her innocent eyes. "Then it is high time we become acquainted," he said in a husky voice.

His lips settled gently on hers for a first tentative taste. A warm wave of tenderness swelled within him. He wanted to love and protect her, and keep her innocent forever. He lifted his head and smiled softly down at her. He felt humbled by the love glowing in her eyes.

She looked a moment, then said shyly, "I am not a child now, Griffin," and wrapped her arms around his neck for a more satisfactory kiss.

The last trace of childhood fell away from her under the impact of that embrace. The memory of his years of loneliness and waiting receded into the recesses of memory, overwhelmed by the here and the now, and the fulfillment of love.

It was a mature woman who returned his ardent embraces, though Alice felt as if she had fallen into a fairy tale from her youth. She had snatched her handsome prince as a prize from the jaws of defeat, and she would never let him go, not for a minute. They would sleep under the stars in a blanket, and pick wildflowers on the cliffs in Greece. What did it matter where they were, as long as they were together? It was some time before they settled down to rational talk.

"I thought you would never realize I had grown up," she said, drawing a luxurious sigh.

"The problem was that I had not grown up, Sal. It was you who pointed out the youthful folly of my ways. I shall try to be a civilized husband."

"Not too civilized," she said coquettishly. "You must remember it was my sister who was afraid of the savage. I loved you just the way you were, Griffin. And I quite look forward to a honeymoon in Greece. I shall sit in the amphitheater, and you shall recite for me—after we have collected all the specimens from the cliffs, I mean."

"I have a year or two of work still to do on my Brazilian trip before going to Greece. We cannot wait that long to marry."

"If I help you, after we are married I mean, perhaps we can finish sooner."

"I have a feeling your help would be too distracting. We shall go in a year or so."

"Griffin, I hope you are not planning to settle down into a dull old scribe. I want to travel."

"So do I, but first I want to marry you."

Echoes of the waltz came from the ballroom. "Let us have a dance at Myra's wedding after all," Griffin suggested.

They rose, and she went into his arms. He held her much more closely than fashion decreed, with both arms around her waist, while she rested her head on his shoulder with her eyes closed, reveling in her newfound happiness.

Mrs. Newbold eventually noticed that Alice was missing from the ballroom and went to look for her. She saw the door of the saloon was ajar, and opened it to see if the servants had tidied up yet. She saw Alice and Griffin moving in slow circles, with such beatific smiles on their faces that she hesitated to interrupt them.

When had that sly puss nabbed Griffin? Mrs. Newbold had no objection to the match; Griffin was well to grass, but how would Myra take it? Ah well, the pair of them would be sheering off to Africa or Peru, very likely, and would not disturb the duchess.

She quietly closed the door and spoke to the butler. "Don't let anyone go into the saloon. The servants have not tidied up yet. It is all at sixes and sevens."

And smelling like April and May, she added to herself. Another wedding to prepare. A mother's work was never done. Yet it would be done once Alice married Griffin. She felt a premonition of loss, until she remembered the future heirs to Dunsmore and Mersham she would soon be dandling on her knee. Then she bustled happily back to the ballroom.

Coming in December 1993
from Fawcett Books.

THE GREAT
CHRISTMAS BALL
by
Joan Smith

Lord Costain's superior at the Horse
Guards is suspected of treason and
Lord Costain is called upon to inves-
tigate. When he enlists the aid of the
charming Miss Lyman as a translator,
he does not expect her to carry out
some very dangerous sleuthing of
her own. Nor does he expect to fall in
love with her.

Look for it in a bookstore
near you.

JOAN SMITH

Call toll free 1-800-733-3000 to order by phone and use your major credit card. Please mention interest code KF-593JS to expedite your order. Or use this coupon to order by mail.

__THE GREAT CHRISTMAS BALL   449-22146-6 $3.99

Name_____

Address_____

City_____State_____Zip _____

Please send me the FAWCETT BOOKS I have checked above.

I am enclosing $_____
   plus
Postage & handling* $_____
Sales tax (where applicable) $_____
Total amount enclosed $_____

*Add $2 for the first book and 50¢ for each additional book.

Send check or money order (no cash or CODs) to Fawcett Mail Sales, 400 Hahn Road, Westminster, MD 21157.

Prices and numbers subject to change without notice.
Valid in the U.S. only.
All orders subject to availability.   KF-593JS